W9-AHK-406

4/14

Tin Star

CECIL CASTELLUCCI

Tin Star

ROARING BROOK PRESS

New York

Published by Roaring Brook Press
Roaring Brook Press is a division of Holtzbrinck Publishing
Holdings Limited Partnership
175 Fifth Avenue, New York, New York 10010
macteenbooks.com

Library of Congress Cataloging-in-Publication Data

Castellucci, Cecil, 1969–
    Tin star / Cecil Castellucci.
       pages cm
    Summary: "Beaten and left for dead, fourteen-year-old Tula Bane finds
herself abandoned on a space station called Yertina Feray after traveling with
the colonist group, Children of the Earth"—Provided by publisher.
    ISBN 978-1-59643-775-3 (hardback)—ISBN 978-1-59643-914-6 (ebook)
    [1. Human-alien encounters—Fiction.   2. Space stations—Fiction.
3. Science fiction.]   I. Title.
    PZ7.C26865Tin 2013
    [Fic]—dc23

                                                        2013002600

Roaring Brook Press books are available for special promotions
and premiums.
For details contact: Director of Special Markets, Holtzbrinck Publishers.

First Edition, 2014
Book design by Andrew Arnold
Printed in the United States of America
1   3   5   7   9   10   8   6   4   2

To the stars! To the stars!
We all make homes among the stars!

1

. . . .

There are few things colder than the blackness of space. But lying here, I couldn't imagine anything colder than the Human heart that left me half-conscious at the entrance to Docking Bay 12.

I knew where I was. I was on a space station called the Yertina Feray, sixteen light years from Earth, orbiting a depleted, lifeless planet. I knew where I was supposed to be, on the Children of Earth colony ship, heading for the planet Beta Granade. And I knew what Brother Blue was thinking, that my body was no longer his problem.

Again I felt his boot come toward me, determined to kick my life away. I braced myself for the blow and then played dead. He kicked me one last time, and satisfied that I was truly gone, he pulled me beside the cargo canisters of grain that had been loaded off our ship, the *Prairie Rose*.

My nose mask had been ripped off, and the station's base atmosphere mix wasn't going to keep me conscious for much longer. I cracked open one of my swollen eyes as much as I dared. I wanted to get a good look at him as he stood there above me, taking a moment to compose himself.

I had gone from being one of his favorite colonists, with prospects for a good future with the Children of Earth, to persona non grata in a matter of days. I never knew a fall could be so quick.

Brother Blue had taken a special interest in me when he discovered that I could speak a passable Universal Galactic. I had always been good at languages. But Brother Blue discouraged colonists from learning Universal Galactic or getting the nanites to make communication and breathing easier.

"We are setting up Human-only colonies," he had said. "You won't be interacting with others. Our mission is to preserve Human ways." He discouraged us all from knowing too much about the galaxy and other cultures. Earth was isolationist, and our colonies would follow suit. We would bring Human culture to the stars and trade with aliens and be richer for it, but we would keep to ourselves. This was Brother Blue's promise.

Brother Blue spent hours telling me his dreams for colonization, flattering me with musings of how high I could rise in the ranks of Children of Earth.

"I'm grooming you, Tula Bane," he said. "You are exactly the kind of person that the Children of Earth needs to help in its cause."

He had this way of making me feel as though I was the only colonist that ever counted. His look was penetrating, and when he spoke of his vision for Humanity, I was ready to sacrifice anything to help him achieve it. I wasn't the only one that felt this way. All of the colonists of the Children of Earth felt as though they had been specially chosen by Brother Blue. It was an honor. Even though I had only reluctantly joined because of my mother's devotion to his cause, I soon felt at one with the group.

When we were diverted to the Yertina Feray due to a ship malfunction, I became even more essential to Brother Blue. He put me to work delivering messages to various aliens that he had to deal with to ensure our ship's repair. I was one of the few colonists who ventured out of the docking bay where we had set up camp. I felt special each time I stepped onto another level of the station.

I imagined my future. It looked so bright. I could be important, perhaps a leader, on our new colony. I imagined rising through the ranks of the Children of Earth. I ran through the colors that I might choose as my name when I had proved my worth. Sister Grey. Sister Lilac. Sister Teal. Sister Gold.

But then something changed.

I had often been sent to Kitsch Rutsok's bar to deliver messages back and forth between Brother Blue and representatives from the League of Worlds; they held the reins to our colony's future. But in the last few days, Brother Blue had gone himself and I wasn't needed.

And today, the day we were to leave the Yertina Feray Space Station, I saw our cargo—cargo that should have been on the ship—sitting on the docking bay floor. This was a terrible oversight. It would be disastrous for our colony if we didn't have the grain we needed to start our new life. The grain was the beginning of how we would tame Beta Granade. Life would already be hard there; and without the cargo, sustaining life would be nearly impossible.

Why were the other colonists not concerned that the grain that we were to plant with was being left behind? Why did no one else notice? I asked my mother, who shrugged.

"Brother Blue knows what he's doing," she said.

My mother used to always argue with my father when he was alive, question him all the time, but she never did with Brother Blue. He was always right in her eyes.

I pointed the grain out to a few others, who seemed unperturbed by the cargo on the deck.

It was as though no one wanted to see it. But it bothered me. It made no sense.

"Sir," I said to one of the ship's officers milling about on deck. "Why is that cargo still out here and not on the ship?"

The young officer turned to look at the cargo and then called over to another officer who shook her head. But at least they agreed with me that it seemed strange.

Brother Blue was called over, and he listened to our concerns with an attentive look. When he'd soothed the officer's worry, he took me over to a private corner.

He had his hand on my shoulder in a way that he had a million times before. Only before it was comforting, encouraging, affectionate. Now it was menacing. He was looking at me and his face was smiling. To anyone looking from afar, he seemed to be pleased with me, but it was just a mask. His attitude shifted from concerned leader to unknowable monster.

"What place do you have to question my orders?" he hissed.

Suddenly I was unsure of myself and of what I knew. Although this was my first and likely only trip into space, I already knew that things could very easily go wrong.

Surely he didn't need me to explain the importance of that cargo to him. I would have thought that he would be happy that I'd noticed. I felt confused by his reaction. Was I wrong?

No. I couldn't be. We were going to be settling a planet. While there were indigenous plants, it could take years before we cataloged what could or couldn't be consumed by Humans. The Children of Earth had a calling: to make a Human oasis among the stars. Our plans for colonization came at a high price, because once we left Earth, we were exiled for good. Earth Gov had a different priority: to rebuild from years of drought and plague. But we of the Children of Earth were certain that in the long run we were doing our best for the future of Humanity, just as those who'd left before in the generational ships had. We needed the grain and the seeds to ensure that future.

"We'll need that grain," I said. "We colonists will need those supplies."

"Tula Bane," he said. "You really are very smart. It's a pity that you don't listen to me."

"But I do listen to you," I said. "I am trying to be helpful. Brother Blue, I'm just trying to learn."

He considered me thoughtfully. His grip on my shoulder was no longer threatening. It was a pat of confidence, just like he used to give me when I had done something right. Relief flooded me. His smile changed to something more genuine. "Child, I hear you. I see you. But do not concern yourself in affairs that you know nothing about," Brother Blue said. "Learn to unlearn."

"Yes, Brother Blue," I said, bowing my head in respect. He had a vision, and he had knowledge that I did not. We all trusted that he knew what was best for us.

"Have I not already helped four Human colonies settle the rocky planets that the League of Worlds has so graciously leased us? Beta Granade will be the fifth," he said. "I know what I'm doing, Tula Bane."

"Of course, Brother Blue," I said. "I didn't mean to question your orders."

"I can see that you didn't," he said. "You were being enthusiastic, but I need you to follow and do what I say."

"Yes, Brother Blue," I said.

"I need you to go to the Brahar ship on Docking Bay 5 and make a delivery."

"But I want to help here," I said, "with the load in." The errand would take me away from the preboarding preparations.

"Do as I ask, Tula," Brother Blue said, and then he flashed that smile. The one that made you feel as though you were the only person in the universe. How could I have ever doubted that Brother Blue knew what he was doing?

"There are plenty of strong bodies to load," Brother Blue assured me.

I had no choice but to obey his wishes as we set about our final preparations. I took a bag heavy with fresh food, salts, and water from Earth to the docking bay with the Brahar ship and gave the bag to the captain. Its value was great. I tried to ignore the desperate aliens who were begging for work near his ship.

"Tell him that she's fueled and ready to go," the Captain said.

I made my way back to join Brother Blue, my family, and the other colonists before reboarding commenced for the final leg of the *Prairie Rose*'s voyage.

I felt relieved to see the docking bay had been cleared. The error had been corrected; I needn't have worried after all. I took a look around the hangar. We were nearly ready to go. I delivered the message to Brother Blue who seemed to understand it. He smiled at me and touched my face.

"Tula, for one so young, you've been such a help to me on this voyage," Brother Blue said coming up to me as I stood with my mother and my sister, Bitty.

"Thank you, Brother Blue," I said, "for the opportunity to be of service."

"We're very proud of her," my mother chimed in.

"Come with me, Tula. I have something for you," he said. "A gift."

"A gift?" I said.

"Good work must be rewarded."

I looked at my mother and sister. They were nervous. My mother did not like space travel although it was she who had decided to move the family off of Earth. Bitty was three years younger than I was and frightened of everything.

"I'd rather stay with my mother and sister," I said.

"I insist," he said.

"It's all right," Mother said. Her pride was showing as the others took notice of the special attention Brother Blue was giving me. She nudged me forward. The higher I rose, the better it would be for all of us. "We'll be fine without you for a little while."

I followed Brother Blue to the hangar's anteroom and there, stacked in the corner, were the bins of grain.

"They're still not onboard," I said.

Surely this time he would explain to me why they were not on the ship.

"You held such promise, Tula. But you have eyes that see in the dark," Brother Blue said. "It's such a disappointment that you had to exhibit this independent streak so late in the game. If I'd seen it earlier, I'd never have taken you under my wing."

"I don't understand," I said.

But instead of answering, it was then that he punched me in the face.

"Why?" I tried to ask, blood filling my mouth.

He hit me again, and now I was too stunned to scream. He did not stop until I was limp. At some point my air mask was knocked off, and the atmosphere of the space station struck me as though it were another blow.

It was only when he thought that I was dead that he moved away from me, into the hangar where the colonists were gathered, leaving me behind the forgotten cargo bins full of grain that had so concerned me.

I wanted to groan, but my lungs ached. I wanted my mother. But I could not call out. I wanted to promise Brother Blue that I would not question his wisdom or mention the cargo bins ever again. But I knew better than to let on that he had not finished the job.

I strained my ears to listen as he gave a speech to his followers.

"Brothers and sisters of Earth! You are on an incredible journey! I envy you as you set out to your new home. Circumstances have forced a change in my plan. I must deal with the politics and datawork that the League of Worlds requires."

He explained that he would instead be heading to Bessen, a moon which served as the capital of the League of Worlds, to consult with the Five Major Species and the other Minor

Species members about new planets that the Children of Earth were bidding for. He would then go back to Earth. He informed the colonists that he had bought a small ship that would leave immediately after the *Prairie Rose* left. I listened to more of his speech, but he did not mention rendezvousing with the colonists on Beta Granade at a later date.

That was a significant change in plan.

Brother Blue always went with the colonists all the way to the planet for first landing day. Only when the first season was through and the colony was deemed as thriving would he go back to Earth to handle the coordinating and recruiting of the next batch of colonists.

There was a collective moan of fear from the colonists. Brother Blue had promised he'd be there with us every step of the way. He had so often told us that he was the only one who could protect us on our journey from the perils of space, from aliens, and from the Humans left over from the generational ships, who'd set out for the stars in the past, settled nowhere, and wandered and roamed. They had grown too wild to join the Children of Earth colonies and were not welcome back on Earth.

I wanted to stand up, but I could not move. And if I did, I was afraid he would surely finish me off. Cowardice kept me quiet.

He continued, hushing them like a soothing father.

"I know, I know. It's disappointing to me as well. But you are the true pioneers! I am envious of your adventure. The first days on a new planet, full of hope and possibility, is my favorite part of the mission to settle the worlds that we aim to call home. I will think of you as the *Prairie Rose* heads to its new planet. And wish you speed and light as you begin to grow and build and make your new home. Although Earth Gov does not appreciate it yet, you are doing a great thing for Humanity. And when times get tough, as we already see they can by our unscheduled stop here, remember that what you do, your courage, your strength, your perseverance, will always be remembered."

There was applause. Then I listened as the colonists began to board the *Prairie Rose*. Brother Blue was likely standing at the entrance to the ship, and I could hear him as he shook hands with every one of the colonists and wished them luck.

Surely my family had noticed by now that I had gone missing. I shifted my body and watched as best I could from behind the crates as my fellow Earthling colonists filed past the anteroom that hid me. They walked in order, as they had been taught. They walked with their heads down, as they had been taught. What I had long suspected was true: We only saw what we were told to see. But now I was seeing something else: Brother Blue was like a magician I'd seen once when I was young, distracting the eye from what he was really doing. I thought back to all of the times that he'd confided in me and realized that they were all tactics to keep me from asking questions. I'd been fooled. The grain had been the last in a long line of things that had bothered me somehow. His words always told a different story, a soothing story, a logical explanation for things that didn't add up. All along I'd known deep down inside that something was not quite right. But I'd been blinded by my desire for a position in the future with Children of Earth. I had been kept in place by not wanting to rock the boat.

I would not make that mistake again.

Though blurry, I watched as Brother Blue approached my mother and sister and heard him say, "Tula will be traveling with me, Mrs. Bane. She's too valuable a right hand man for me to give her up now."

"Yes, Brother Blue," she said. "We're so happy for her prospects."

"She'll rise very high under my tutelage."

And there it was. No one would suspect that it could be otherwise. My family would never know or have cause to believe that he would lie.

Brother Blue stayed until the last colonist was onboard. He stayed until the docking door swung and clicked shut with a hiss of air. He waited until the sound of the ship unclamping from the station came. Only then did he walk away. From where I lay, I could see that he did not look disturbed that he had just broken his word to the 167 colonists in his care. He looked relieved.

And then he was gone.

No one would care about a dead body on the docking bay. I'd seen plenty of them. They were robbed and then disposed of by the rabble of aliens who looked for work on the few ships that docked.

But I was not dead yet.

I tried to adjust my weight again to make some of the pain stop, and then dragged myself out of the anteroom to the hangar, as though I could somehow catch up with the ship before it left the station. But it was too late. They were gone. What was I to do now? My eyes caught sight of the *Prairie Rose* as it sailed by the window in the hangar. It moved so slowly that at first it didn't seem as though it was leaving at all. It was only when it began to shrink in size against the blackness of space that I was sure that it was leaving me behind. The *Prairie Rose* sailed on its edge, looking like a thin silver line; when it reached acceleration, it flipped up, ready to slingshot around the nearby depleted planet below and shoot out of the system in a light skip.

It was a sight to see.

The ship had five shiny points, its metal glinting in the glare of the weak sun. It looked like a tin star, the kind I had seen in history books, the kind that officers of the law wore. I managed to lift my hand, as though to touch the ship, before it vanished from sight.

Then, the ship was gone, and so was my family.

They had all left me here, on the floor of the Yertina Feray space station.

That knowledge—that I was utterly alone—felt sharper than the beating. It made the pain in my body intolerable.

Everything—the hangar, the window, and the ship's fading streak of silver—went black.

2

. . . .

Unconsciousness did not last long.

It was the pain that woke me. My body ached. My lungs burned. My eyes were swollen shut. I was aware of some aliens moving around me. If I had the standard-issue nanites swimming inside of me, I would have been able to breathe the station's base atmosphere: the nanites would have worked to adjust the mix my Human body needed by assimilating the gases that my lungs couldn't process. Some nanites would have made their way to my brain to attach themselves to my cerebral cortex, working with my current language skills to improve and provide better translation of Universal Galactic when it was being spoken.

All at once, one of the aliens let out a noise, and I knew that I'd been discovered.

I stayed as still as I could.

I felt a poke. Then another poke.

I had heard somewhere that if you did not know who was around you, it was always best to play dead. Doing so had already saved me. It did not take them long to see that I had nothing on me to steal. After that, I was someone else's problem and so they stopped prodding me and went back to their business of taking the grain that was supposed to be seeded on a new planet. *My* new planet. But I was helpless. All I could do was listen in frustration as the creatures spoke in their native language among themselves.

As they left with the cargo, I wondered if Earth grains were valuable to other species. It dawned on me that Brother Blue had perhaps sold the grain to these aliens for profit.

I lost consciousness again and awoke later to discover more aliens surrounding me. I willed myself to understand what the aliens were saying. I concentrated. I still had so much Universal Galactic to learn.

I was certain that they were talking about me. Perhaps negotiating over my body. That made me frightened. Maybe it was true that aliens harvested Humans. That was the rumor on Earth. My interactions with aliens so far made me not believe it. We Humans were disliked, it was true, but this was because of the Human wanderers. We colonists were different than they were, and I had seen no evidence that aliens were the monsters that Brother Blue or ignorant Earthlings said they were.

"Dead?" I understood that word, it was said by the one who seemed to be in charge.

When my mother first committed us to becoming colonists on the *Prairie Rose*, I would often steal away to the library and listen to all the data reels of Universal Galactic I could find. I had learned some in spite of the language's difficulties, but the accents were tricky and varied. Meaning could be altered by an inflection or a pitch.

I only understood snippets of what the other alien said. I could tell from his clicks and thrums that he was a bug-like creature. The clicks and thrums made his Universal Galactic even harder to understand without the nanites.

". . . not an expert on Human . . . from the state of it . . .

usually one solid color . . . blues and reds and yellows . . .
puffiness . . . normal . . . eyes are closed . . . sleep or
death . . ."

It was too hard. I wanted to be where I should be—in a
bunk on a colony ship—uncomfortable, but heading toward
a new home on Beta Granade with my family. If I had not
made myself so useful to Brother Blue with my limited language skills, then I could have soon been standing on a new
planet, with dirt in my hands, planting seeds, building a new
home. Instead, I was crumpled and broken on a cold space
station floor.

As I struggled to follow the conversation happening above
me, I couldn't help but think that not giving the translator
and breathing nanites to the colonists or letting us learn
Universal Galactic was another way for Brother Blue to keep
us all under control. If we could not understand, then we
could do nothing but follow. I was too inquisitive. I had always been so. My father had said it was a gift. My mother
had warned me when we joined the Children of Earth to
keep it in check.

The aliens were speaking quickly and using slang, so I
couldn't be sure of anything I was hearing but finally I was
able to follow again.

"You weren't working the docks, looking for work?" the
one with the more melodic voice said.

"No . . . Humans came at once . . . Ship . . . airlock . . .
the way that they sound . . . vibration . . . voices . . . my
ears . . . I left . . . they were gone . . . cargo . . . others . . .
then nothing . . . gone . . ."

I tried to open my eyes; they barely moved, but through
the blur I could see a few of the aliens as they moved toward

me. Pain flooded my body as they lifted me onto a stretcher. This was my only chance to do something. My tongue felt too swollen to form words. I wasn't even sure that I would be understood. But I had to try.

"Wait," I said in thick Universal Galactic. "Wait."

To my ears it sounded less like a word and more like an undead moan.

"Ahhh!" the bug-like alien screamed. "That frequency! Terrible. I hate them. I hate Humans."

"That thing is alive," the other alien said. He was leaning in very closely to me. He was looking in my eyes, touching my skin, and he felt that I was still warm. He was a Loor, one of the Major Species. I could tell by his antennae. They were folded toward my face, almost touching my skin. "Get the doctor."

I could feel the aliens' mood change. Whereas before they were just doing their job, they now moved around with new urgency. I sank back into the stretcher. I'd announced myself. Everyone I knew in the Children of Earth said that aliens were not to be trusted. But it was out of my hands now. They would either finish me off, or save me.

The Loor put a nose mask on my face, and when the air hit me, I could breathe easier. It felt sweet. My mind cleared, and I was better able to follow the Universal Galactic.

"I'll have to contact the Earth representative at the League of Worlds," the Loor said. "That means datawork."

"Do they even have one?" I heard someone else ask. "I thought they were isolationists?"

"Things are always changing with these Minor Species," the Loor said.

"Too bad it's not dead," the bug-like creature said. I wondered if he saw me as a meal.

"If the body had fallen a bit closer to the waste disposal, I would have pushed it in and been rid of it. I don't like to deal with the Humans," the Loor said.

"They are a mostly unknown species."

"But they're always roaming."

The doctor came and examined me. I kept still on the gurney.

"Alive," the doctor said. "Alive."

"Bring it to the med bay," the one in charge said.

I felt the stretcher lift up and move. After hours of darkness and pain, I could feel the tiniest spark of life in me.

• •

I awoke, submerged partway in a tank of warm water, surrounded by thousands of tiny water creatures. The water was warm, and the creatures came and kissed my skin. After the cold of the *Prairie Rose*, the floor of the cargo bay, the tasteless food, and the endless boredom of the voyage, I finally felt something akin to contentment. For a moment, I could almost believe that someone had come to help me and thus, the universe had answered my call.

The tank was perfectly adjusted for Human atmosphere and gravity. I floated. It was too blissful. I wondered how far along the *Prairie Rose* was on its journey. I wondered how long it would take me to catch up to them. I wondered if my family missed me as much as I missed them.

I opened my eyes. Through the tank I could see three aliens. Two were in beds. One was holding an instrument. I recognized her—although I couldn't really be sure of the gender—as the doctor who had declared me alive.

She had four arms, a pointy chin, and a pointy head. The doctor was extremely thin, like a walking stick. She had one of her hands on the forehead of the patient in the bed, another entering something onto a keypad, while another was tapping her hip. I recognized her from my studies as a Per, another one of the Major Species. As a Human, I was considered a Minor Species, or maybe even less than Minor. The difference between Major and Minor had to do with how long you'd been a spacefaring race and how many colonies a civilization had out in the stars. You had to have more than a dozen to be considered Major.

The doctor noticed that I was awake, and she took her free hand and through a flap in the tank wall injected me with a hypo. I slid back to sleep, peacefully dreaming of stars and the colony that I would help build.

· ·

I felt warm. Where was I again?

Perhaps the hand that pressed on my forehead was my mother's hand. Perhaps I had just been sick. Gotten a flu or eaten something disagreeable. Perhaps I was already there on Beta Granade, in a fevered sweat. Perhaps everything else that had happened that I was suddenly remembering had only been a nightmare.

Perhaps.

I opened my eyes again and saw the door slide open. An alien in a uniform came in. It was the Loor, the most Human-looking of all the alien species. They were taller and thinner with longer extremities than Humans. They had broad shoulders, short necks, and thick antennae on the tops of their heads. Between the antennae and above the small hairline was a small widow's peak of pale skin. The color varied from Loor to Loor. I recognized him when he spoke as the alien who was giving orders when they found me and declared me alive.

Seeing him reminded me that I was still on the Yertina Feray. I had only been dreaming that everything was fine. I had only been wishing. I closed my eyes to make my reality untrue for a moment longer.

"How is she? Is she able to talk?" he asked.

"The patient is making adequate progress but is not yet all better," the doctor said.

"When can she leave here?"

I could feel the weight of his glare through the envirotank. I listened.

"Perhaps soon," the doctor said.

"You've been saying that for weeks now and yet, here she still is."

"Humans, very tricky. I am not familiar with their recovery times. I am doing the best I can. As you know, we're a sparsely populated station and I do not have an adequate staff."

"Release her tomorrow and send her to me," he said.

He left the room. The last of the warmth I felt from the dream slipped away. I opened my eyes and saw the doctor as she came over to me with an injection.

"No," I said. "No."

The doctor smiled and put one of her hands through the flap and placed it on my head, stroking me, as though I were a dog or a cat, and then I felt the prick of a needle.

"You have a little fight in you," the doctor said. "No matter what species, that is always a good sign."

"Something is wrong," I said thickly, hoping my accent was acceptable as I slid into unconsciousness.

"Yes, but I do not know the details. And now it seems as though there is nothing more that I can do for you, Human."

"Tula," I said. "My name is Tula."

The doctor smiled and then moved away. Whatever care she had given, she was done now. I was here on my own.

3

• •

Constable Tournour's office was bright, white, and spare. He sat at his desk, empty of anything except for a single, small, flowering plant, which I knew from my limited exposure to space travel was a sign of wealth. Plants on a space station were rare, except in arboretums. Perhaps it was a payoff. It didn't matter. It meant that though he was a low-ranking constable, he had power.

Behind him, through the window, I could see the planet that the Yertina Feray station was orbiting had come into view. I'd forgotten the planet's name but knew that it was smaller than Earth. It was a sickly gray color except for a strange rust-colored belt around its center on one of the continents. All I remembered was that whatever had been mined there in the past had long ago been depleted. The planet was inhospitable. No one lived there. No one mined there anymore. It used to be the reason why this station was so important. Now it was the reason why the Yertina Feray was on a little-used trade route. No one came here, unless they were lost or in trouble.

We had been detoured here with mechanical difficulties. What was it Brother Blue had said? *An unexpected glitch.*

Until Constable Tournour began speaking in rapid Universal Galactic, he seemed almost familiar. It wasn't just that the Loor carried themselves the same as Humans, it was that their eyes were not so alien as the others' were. Of course, his antennae and lack of eyebrows brought home the fact that Tournour was not at all Human.

"Please speak slowly," I said. "I have no nanites."

Tournour stared at me. He squared his broad shoulders. And then he began again slowly.

"You'd have been better off dead," he said.

"I don't think I agree with that," I said.

"You will," he said.

I said nothing. He intimidated me. I couldn't look at him, so I looked at the plant and its yellow flower. It was brighter than the yellow suns I used to draw when I was a little girl.

"No one claims that you are missing," Tournour said.

"I came here with the Children of Earth colonists on the *Prairie Rose*; we were heading to Beta Granade when we ran into engine trouble. We were docked here for repairs. You must have seen us on the station."

It took me forever to form the words. Tournour was patient as he watched me struggle to speak.

"Yes, we saw the Humans." Tournour made a face. It was a face that I was beginning to recognize; one of distaste for my species.

"And yet no one seems to admit that you exist. The Children of Earth claim to have never heard of you and therefore have no place for you on any of their four colonies. They also say all life forms are accounted for on the *Prairie Rose* and that you are not on that manifest. Earth, as you know, does not extend protection to those who choose to leave."

"You are talking too fast," I said.

He repeated himself.

"They left me behind," I said.

"No one wants you," Tournour said.

"My family wants me."

"They have a funny way of showing it," Tournour said.

"There's been a mistake," I said. "A misunderstanding."

Tournour looked frustrated. I noticed that his skin patch turned darker as though he were flushed.

"Well, whatever the problem is, it's no longer mine. We are no longer responsible for you," he said.

"What will I do?" I asked.

"You can try to appeal," Tournour said. "We can no longer afford to extend any hospitality to you. As I said, you are Human and not our problem."

"Where will I go?" I asked.

"That's the trouble with Humans, you think that the rules of the universe don't apply to you and that you can wander anywhere. You travel and roam from place to place. Nomads. You fight against each other instead of working together."

"I don't know anything about that," I said. "I just want to catch up with my mother and sister and head to the Human colony on Beta Granade."

Tournour's antenna folded and straightened.

"Do you have any friends on the station?" he asked.

"No. What's left of my family and friends are on the *Prairie Rose*."

"Do you have a currency chit?"

"No."

Tournour paused.

"How old are you?"

"Fourteen," I said. "Almost fifteen."

"Is that old or young?" Tournour asked. "It's hard to tell with some species."

"Young."

"Are you a child?"

"I don't think so," I said.

"That's a shame. If you were an actual child, then maybe I could find a loophole. There are more lenient rules regarding children."

It was hard to read aliens, but it seemed to me that this one had softened.

I didn't feel like a child. I was only months away from the age of majority. At 15 I could legally emancipate myself, even if I was not allowed to vote or marry or imbibe.

"Are you old or young?" I asked.

I could tell that I had surprised him. It pleased me a little bit that I could. It made the moment seem more real, rather than surreal, which was how I'd felt since the med bay released me and sent me here.

"Why would you care?" He seemed defensive. His antennae turned from left to right quickly. I'd agitated him.

"I'm just curious," I said.

"I don't know what your species considers old or young," Tournour said, relaxing. "I haven't met very many Humans. I'm not very well traveled."

"You're here," I said.

"So are you," he said and then paused. "I'm more than less."

I didn't understand what that meant. I knew that some species considered fifty years old to still be a child. No matter how hard Humans had tried to extend longevity, it was rare for anyone to be older than 115.

"Where will I go?" I asked.

"I don't know."

"Who can I ask for help?"

His antennae folded and pointed at me. Then they stood back up straight.

"There is always the Ministry of Colonies and Travel," he said.

"What's that?"

"Since only the five Major Species have embassies, the Ministry of Colonies and Travel is for everyone else with grievances. A place for colonists from Minor Species, or those below that, aliens with only home planets and no colonies at all. Every Minor Species always has something to grieve about. But you need to purchase a token to do a search."

"I don't have any currency," I said. "I don't have anything."

"You are no longer the Yertina Feray's responsibility. I don't want to see you again. So stay out of trouble. And disappear."

I stood there, not quite knowing if that meant I was dismissed. Suddenly, my feet would not move. This was not a dream that I would awaken from. Brother Blue really meant to leave me behind. Worse, he thought I was dead. No one I cared about knew that I was not OK. I had nowhere to go and no one to turn to. *Nothing.*

No clear thoughts formed in my head on what to do next. There were no other Humans here to ask for help. Humans had never had a presence on this station, something I had learned while walking around, helping Brother Blue. The colonists had been the first Humans on the Yertina Feray in decades.

I was the only one of my species here.

Perhaps this constable was right. It would have been easier if I had died.

I screamed.

Tournour cocked his head to the side and his antennae moved wildly on his head. I felt embarrassed as he watched me melt down, but I could not stop. Tears came. A moment before, I had felt old enough, but maybe it was not too late to admit that I was still a child. Perhaps a loophole was my best bet.

But before I could beg, Tournour spoke again.

"I am going to turn around now and look at the planet, Quint. I am going to stare at it for a minute or two."

Quint. That was the planet's name.

"When I turn back you will be gone," he continued. "I will not miss you. Nor will I notice anything of value that might be missing from this room."

Tournour turned around. I looked around the room. There was a token on the desk. There were strange rocks on a shelf. Perhaps jewels. There were datapads. Perhaps electronics were valuable? But my eyes kept going back to the plant with the yellow flower. I stepped forward and snatched the plant and the token and ran out of the room just as Tournour was turning back around.

I could use the token to do a search. My family was likely on Beta Granade by now, and the first thing the colonists would do would be to set up a communications beacon.

I wandered the station until I found the Ministry of Colonies and Travel. The many empty sectors of the station hinted at its former glory: the grand hotels, the closed entertainment centers, the Sunspa, the places of worship that almost no one attended. Most of the levels were sealed off to save costs. Only a small part of the station was fully operational.

I knew that I did not look presentable, but there was nothing I could do about that. Once I reached my family, they could transmit enough currency to help me rejoin them. I kept reminding myself that although I felt alone, I did belong somewhere.

I was a Human colonist from Beta Granade.

Until I reached my mother, I would have to wait it out alone on the station. Perhaps it would be a few months before they would be able to make arrangements. I thought a few months might be bearable with the promise of a reunion at the end of it.

I was sitting patiently in the waiting room when a receptionist, a fat round alien with an enormous head, small extremities, and two mouths came out.

"Tula Bane," he called. His voice sounded like a chord played on a piano, high and low tones at the same time. It was pure music.

I stood up and smoothed my dirty clothes as best I could to look my best when I talked to my family.

The receptionist began to speak quickly. The music ceased. One mouth was talking, agitated. The other one was frowning. I stopped him.

"What did you just say?" I asked.

"The *Prairie Rose* never made it to Beta Granade," the alien said. "A trace shows that it disintegrated on its light skip into that system. All life forms were lost. It happens all the time. Many colonists never make it to the planet, and if they do, they often don't make it past the first year alive. So hard to become a Major Species."

27

The alien turned away. He did not say *I'm sorry for your loss*. Or, *Is there anything we can do to help you?* He just turned away and called on another waiting alien.

My family was dead. They weren't going to come for me. There was no help to ask for. There would be no happy reunion. Not ever. I wondered if that's what Tournour was trying to tell me when he'd said, "all life forms accounted for." I wondered if his confusing kindness was meant to tell me to sell the token to someone else for currency.

I stumbled out of the Ministry of Colonies and Travel. Aliens pushed by me on their way to the Sunspa or to the market or to their place of work. They all had somewhere to be.

I could not think of a single place to go next.

4

. . . .

When you are lost, go back to the beginning. **That's**
what my father always told me when I was a little girl. I remembered his canvas coveralls, thick and stiff when he would
come home from the factory. I would be confused about
homework, or having trouble following my grandmother's
senile logic. He'd pull me up on his lap and tell me to go back
to the beginning, and sure enough, a thread would be there
for me to follow.

I wished that he were alive now. If I had known then that
his death would lead me here to this moment, I would have
begged my mother to stay on Earth. If he were alive then
maybe my mother wouldn't have joined the Children of
Earth, and we would be safe at home. I could have been
happy on Earth. I could have been happy in the small garden
my father and I tried to grow. I could have been happy looking
at the stars and keeping them far away. I wanted my family
back.

Right now I would have settled for any Human, just to
have someone familiar to ask for help from. But I was the
only one of my kind. I wanted to stop and fall down every
time I reminded myself that.

Movement meant survival. So I kept moving.

The station was big, but my feet moved quickly and

covered a lot of ground, past the stores on the shopping quarter and the sleeping quarters and station operations. I went up and up and up in the elevators until I reached the docking bays. I didn't stop until I reached Docking Bay 12. I must have stood there and stared at it for hours, thinking that the *Prairie Rose* would somehow return and retrieve me, even though that would never happen. I could only think magically now. Reality would crush me.

Nothing happened. No ship docked. Not many aliens were around. For a docking bay, there was very little action. But that was the way that it was on the whole station.

I went now to the anteroom and sat down with my stolen plant. I imagined entering the airlock and opening it and falling out of the station and into the darkness of space. Everything about my thoughts was ugly.

But the plant in front of me was beautiful. And while my thoughts were numb, my eyes fixed on the yellow of the blooms.

It kept me from doing something that could not be undone.

• •

"How much do you want for the plant?"

I opened my eyes to see a large insect-like alien. I remembered him from the day I was found.

"It's not for sale," I said. My voice cracked. My throat was dry, and the air mask the med bay had issued me itched. It was losing its ability to filter air. I wish they had given me the nanites, but I could not afford them and they were not automatically given, especially to Humans. And even though I was thirsty and hungry and I hadn't eaten in days. I knew that if I lost the plant, I would lose the war waging inside of me. The plant meant life.

The alien made a noise.

"Oh, you Human, don't speak! You are trying to kill me with your sounds."

I wasn't sure where his eyes were. I chose to focus on the two protuberances on the side of his head. That seemed to work. He pointed at the plant again.

"How much?"

"It's not for sale," I whispered in the Universal Galactic my dizzy brain could remember.

The alien's face changed. Perhaps he was smiling. Perhaps he was angry. I could not tell. He rearranged himself, and his tiny wings fluttered for a moment.

"There, talk low like that and I won't steal it from you. Instead, we can negotiate. My name is Heckleck."

"Tula Bane," I croaked.

"I'd like your plant," Heckleck said.

I looked at my plant, knowing that I should sell it. The plant was the only thing I owned. It was the only beautiful thing in the cargo bay and though it would probably save me to sell it, I could not let it go.

"I'll give you a hot meal and some currency on your chit," Heckleck said.

I pulled the plant closer to me and crossed my arms around it on the ground in front of me as though I were guarding it behind a wall. I could see by his movements that he wanted the plant very much. It was probably worth more than he was offering.

"No," I whispered.

"Did you say *no*?" Heckleck asked. "Your Universal Galactic is terrible."

I shook my head from side to side.

"Yes. Good. Good to do business with you," he said reaching for the plant.

I pulled the plant up into my arms and cradled it.

"I said NO!" I shouted. It used up the last of my energy. I was blind with hunger. I was wiped.

Heckleck groaned in pain and then all I could see was his mouth coming toward me. He extruded his tongue, which looked like a sharp pointy barb, and injected my arm. I dropped the plant and tried to scramble away. I felt the barb sting my arm and immediately I felt nauseous. I looked back at Heckleck. He was not reaching for the plant; instead, he was calmly looking at me, rubbing his little wings, which made a mournful sound.

My head ached, and I felt hot. Had Heckleck killed me? Perhaps he was like an insect on Earth, calmly waiting for paralysis to set in before he finished me off at his leisure, picking off parts of me when needed. If I had been agreeable, I could have lived.

But maybe it was for the best that he'd killed me.

Maybe it was better that he ended my life over a pretty plant. Maybe this insect-like alien had done me a kindness. After all, I had just thought about killing myself and had been too cowardly to do it.

I looked around the cargo bay. Through the window, I could see that we'd rotated back, making Quint, the planet below, visible. I figured I would fix my gaze on it. Staring at it while I died would be like sending a hopeful wish out to the universe. It was an image to hang on to. At least I'd gone somewhere. At least I'd seen something extraordinary. A whole other world. A different sun.

The station PA system blared, as it always had, the announcer speaking too quickly for me to understand. I began to sweat profusely. The ringing in my ears became louder until I thought it would make my head explode, and then everything seemed to pause. I felt clear; my breathing became easier, and the words spilling forth from the PA began to make more precise sense:

"Station Time 1800 hours. Full newscast available on the O-ring. Remember to always wash your extremities for health safety. Current station alert is yellow."

I looked around surprised.

"What's going on?" I said. My head had a sharp pain, which then subsided. I could feel my brain changing.

"It's working. Good," Heckleck said. "So, what do you want for the plant?"

There was a slight delay, like an echo in my brain, but then I could understand him perfectly. There was no accent.

"You stabbed me!" I said. I was forming words in Universal Galactic naturally, almost as though I had spoken it fluently, instead of haltingly, my whole life.

"Oh, don't be ridiculous. I injected you with some of my nanites so I could understand you," Heckleck said. "I'm glad I did; the nonaltered frequency of your voice was just about killing me."

"I feel strange," I said.

But I could understand him in a more precise way than I had before he'd stabbed me. And more important, I could now breathe freely without the mask. I ripped it off of my

33

face and threw it to the ground. Without it binding me, I felt curiously free.

"The nanites are reproducing. Just calm down. Try to breathe normally. Relax. Once they reach their maximum, your body will normalize. Right now they are multiplying."

"Do you sting many people?" I asked.

"Usually I sting to kill, not to talk," he said. "But no, I don't do that very often."

I didn't feel relieved.

"You may experience some discomfort. Sorry about that; it's hard to know how a species will react. I've never stung a Human before. I suppose we can be glad it didn't kill you. Although then I'd have the plant for free. Now, what do you want for this plant?"

"I want to go home," I said.

Heckleck laughed. Or at least he made a noise that I thought could have been a laugh.

"The plant is not worth that," Heckleck said. "Besides, it's not like the old days anymore."

"I want to go home," I said again. Not knowing even where that would be.

"Don't you pay attention to the announcements? There's been a coup. The League of Worlds has been dismantled and now the Major Species have joined together in the Central Systems under the jurisdiction and protection of the Imperium."

"What's the Imperium?" I asked.

It must have been a trick of the light because I could have sworn that this alien insect creature looked wistful for a moment.

"I just care about Earth," I said.

"Well that's exactly why the Imperium has seized power; because enough species don't care."

He looked at me and then at the plant. He began to rub his wings, which filled the docking bay with an eerie sound.

"The plant. What's it worth?" I asked.

"If I return it to the constable, he'll give me a favor."

That didn't make the plant seem as though it was worth much at all.

"I need help to get off the station," I said. But even as I clung to that idea, I knew that there were not many ways off of the Yertina Feray, and fewer ways back to Earth, especially when they wouldn't take me back.

"I know about you," Heckleck said. "Everyone does. And you will never get off this station. You are nobody. And worse, you're a Human. Even if you did get on a ship that would take one of your kind, you'd have nowhere to go but to roam like the others of your kind do. And it would cost you more currency chits than you'd likely make in a hundred years."

"There are other colonies that the Children of Earth have built. I'll go to one of those."

But I was not certain that I would be welcomed. The Children of Earth kept to themselves and Brother Blue had shown me that I was not one of them anymore.

"Didn't you hear me? Perhaps your nanites are not yet working. Humans roam and wander. They are not settlers. They are a burden to everyone."

"We Humans are just starting to settle the stars," I said. "But we're out there."

I pointed to the window, to indicate the stars and space.

Quint was still visible, and it had rotated and I could now

see a mountain range. I leaned toward it, as though I were a part of it; as though that planet would claim me, even though no one was down there. As I did, the plant fell to its side and some of the soil spilled onto the floor. I began to scoop what I could and put it back into the pot. It felt good to have dirt on my hands.

"Listen to me carefully," he said. "You are taking up water and food that the Yertina Feray is already sadly low on. With you dead it will mean more for those with nowhere to go. More scraps for those who have been thrown away."

"Then do that why don't you?" I said. "Sit there and watch me die."

He looked as though he were going to move across the cargo bay and do just that. Instead he settled his body down on the floor next to me.

"Do you know how many species survive in your situation on this station? Almost none. They come in on a ship, in trouble or troubled. They come out here to find work that doesn't exist, or to disappear to the Outer Rim thinking they'll find something better, or a new world to settle. But there aren't that many viable planets to settle. No currency to get there if they do find somewhere. No allies. No friends. No help. Nothing. Do you know how many aliens like you I have watched die? Scores."

I knew what he was saying was true. I wanted to cry, but instead I hardened myself.

"But I'm feeling generous today," Heckleck said. "Give me the plant and I will owe you a favor."

"Favors are useless if I'm dead. Besides, how can I trust you?"

"You can't," Heckleck said. "I'm not a nice Hort."

I laughed. It was not funny, but somehow having a conversation with someone felt normal after being so isolated.

"Are you strong enough to run an errand for me?" Heckleck asked. "If you are, then I will pay you in currency loaded onto this chit. I do not go to the social level often; the noise is too much for my kind when it is most crowded, even with the nanite frequency adjustments. But I have to deliver this package to a ship captain who likes to get drunk at Kitsch Rutsok's bar when he's in port. Deliver it and bring back the item he gives you, and I'll pay you then."

"Pay me first," I said.

"This is why the universe is at such odds with itself. No one trusts anyone!" Heckleck said handing me a chit. "Fine. Here is payment. If you run off with it, so be it. I'll find your dead body eventually and retrieve the item, the chit, and the plant."

Heckleck took a wrapped-up linen package the size of a sandwich roll out from under one of his chest plates and pressed it into my hands. The linen was wet with a grayish color.

"What is this?" I asked.

"It's a digit from one of his crew members. Tell him to give you the item, or I'll send the rest of the crew members to him in pieces."

I realized the grayish substance was likely the alien's blood.

I looked over Heckleck's shoulder out the window, at the planet and beyond it to the stars.

I stood up.

If I was going to survive and get off of this station, I would have to trust him. I felt dizzy, my stomach grumbled. I had to eat. It had been too long. I was afraid that if I took the plant with me I would lose it. It was safer here.

I placed the plant in front of Heckleck.

"If I find that you have betrayed me in any way, I will summon up all of my strength and use it to kill you," I said.

"Then we have an agreement," Heckleck said.

I nodded and then stumbled out of the cargo bay.

I would do it. I would live.

5

. . . .

Kitsch Rutsok's bar was as crowded as a place on an
empty space station could be. Still, since hardly any ships
docked on the Yertina Feray, it was not hard to spot the captain that Heckleck wanted me to give the digit to. He was a
blobby sort of creature who was red all over his body, with
enormous arms and hands and, most likely due to the difference of gravity that he was used to, he floated on a hover
seat. He was gesticulating and shouting as he played a game
of chance that looked like roulette. There were two females
of his species hanging on to him. Every time he won a round
they moved their seats from side to side and bumped in a
little closer to each other.

I went to the bar and looked at the menu. I knew from
having run my errands for Brother Blue that not much on the
menu was actual food. Real food and nonrecycled water were
rare and expensive. The bulk of the menu was different kinds
of protein paks similar to what we had been rationed to eat
on the *Prairie Rose*. The variety offered was to cater to the
different nutritional needs of different kinds of aliens. At this
point for me, being so malnourished, anything would do.
The barkeep came over to me, and I pointed to a random item
and presented the currency chit. The barkeep ran my chit
through.

"Sorry, Human. This chit says pending. It needs to be authorized. Come back in a few hours."

Heckleck had cheated me. Or rather, he had ensured that I would do the job before I did anything else. My stomach growled. I felt faint. But hunger has a way of energizing a person. I pushed through the crowd to confront the blobby captain.

"Move out of my way," he said as I squeezed in front of him, hitting my side with his hovering seat.

"Heckleck told me to give you this," I said, presenting him with the bloodied linen.

The captain bumped me with his hover seat, pushing me aside to place another bet.

I was too hungry and too tired to deal with being ignored. I threw the linen onto the gaming table. When it landed, the digit rolled out and onto a number.

"No more bets," the game master called.

Everyone fell silent when they saw the body part on the table with the gambling chips.

The captain turned to me.

"Tell Heckleck he can go jump out an air lock."

"Number 24," the game master said. "The number is 24."

The captain and his companions uttered a noise. I didn't know if it was because they lost the bet, were horrified at the bloody digit, or if they were simply laughing at me. I knew from my rounds with Brother Blue that most ships that came here were small and every crew person essential. The Yertina Feray was not a station where you could easily replace someone, and running a ship without a full complement could mean your death. I watched as he placed another bet. And then I took my own gamble.

"What does your crew member do?" I said. "Probably something important. Can you really do without him?"

The color drained from the captain's face. His skin went from red to almost pig-pink.

"Tell Heckleck I'll bring him what he wants," the captain said, and turned back to the game.

"No," I said.

"You are just an errand boy," the captain said, not able to tell that I was a Human girl. "Deliver the message and leave."

"I haven't eaten, and I won't get paid until I bring the package to him," I said.

The captain sighed. He picked up the digit from the table and indicated for me to follow him. I tried not to lose him as he glided. He brought me to the guest quarters and made me wait outside his room. Just when I thought he would never come out again and that he had somehow evaded me, he emerged with a piece of metal that looked like a gear and a small wooden box.

"Here," he said. "Tell Heckleck to let my man go and that our business is done. Tell him I owe him nothing now."

I took the items and made my way back down to Docking Bay 12, where I had left Heckleck and the plant. The box vibrated, as though it were alive with energy. I wondered what was inside.

"That was fairly speedy," Heckleck said when I arrived. "I expected it to take you a few days."

"You didn't pay me," I said. "I couldn't eat. I shouldn't have trusted you."

"I told you not to trust me," Heckleck said. "You'll find that your chit works now. I'll add a little extra since you did it in record time. Meanwhile, you must be starved. Share this snack with me."

Heckleck opened the box. The inside was slithering with what looked like maggots. Heckleck dipped what passed for a finger into the box, and the maggots clung to him like writhing honey. He sucked them off his digit and closed what I thought of as his eyes in what looked like delicious satisfaction.

"What is that?" I asked. Looking at them sickened me. But my stomach growled as I watched Heckleck eat.

"It's a delicacy of my planet," he said.

"And what's that?" I pointed to the gear.

"That's how I cobble together my pitiful existence here," he said. "I barter things for things and favors for favors. That captain needed his cargo unloaded and sold, which I did for him quickly and quietly in exchange for that gear which another client of mine needs. This treat was my bonus."

"You're a thief," I said.

"No, I never steal," he said. "But sometimes I persuade. Don't worry, that digit I took will grow back. His species regenerates them."

My stomach growled again as he offered the box to me.

"You see, I'm not so different from you," Heckleck said. "I am stuck here just as you are. I would have died, unless someone had helped me. I suppose it is just my turn to help a fellow gutter dweller."

"Actually, you are pretty different from me," I said. I was certain that we were nothing alike. I would wager that not even anything in our DNA could be similar.

He offered the box to me again. I could not be picky. I dipped my fingers into the box. The maggots clung to my fingers like leeches, and when I popped them into my mouth, they crunched. My body was grateful, and although looking at them sickened me, I forced them down.

They tasted like sweet potatoes.

6

. . . .

The longer I was stranded, the more I lost all of my feelings except for one.

Numb.

I was numb. If you asked me, I could not remember if a week or a month or a year had gone by. There was only making it to the next day. I could only remember to fight for my life. There was only one rule I lived by: Survive.

I tried to get used to my new reality.

I lived in the very bottom of the Yertina Feray with the others who had nowhere to go and no way to leave. I did not have a home, per se; it was more like I had a bin. I didn't mind squatting in the underguts because it meant that every currency chit I earned I kept. I was interested in leaving, not making a home here.

But the underguts were not an easy place to live. It was dirty and dark and there were noises that I could not identify, which on my first nights scared me. The only noise that did not frighten me was the familiar knock of Heckleck's appendage against the side of my bin.

I preferred not to know most of what Heckleck dealt in. I was just his errand girl. I knew that Heckleck dealt in the more shady areas of trade, finding the things that no one else

wanted to. He had no problem with the dark and the per-
verse. The fact that I had excelled in that first errand had
made me invaluable, but he never asked me to do something
with body parts ever again. Not knowing about the darker
parts of his business was the only way that I could bear to be
in his company. He respected my feelings about that, and
whatever the bulk of his dealings were he did not speak of
them with me. It was a silence between us; a silence that always stretched to the limit of what was acceptable between
two people who still only cautiously called each other friend.
But a silence that allowed us to have trust.

So he spoke to me about the small things that seemed
unimportant. Things that my heart could handle. The gossip
overheard in Kitsch Rutsok's bar. The quality of the harvest
in the arboretum. The varieties and kinds of waters and salts
he'd traded that day. The amount of time he'd logged in the
Sunspa.

"We're in for a treat tomorrow," he said as we walked
through the arboretum. "There's to be a hocht."

"What's a hocht?"

I still had so much to learn about the Yertina Feray and
living among aliens.

"Ah, a hocht," Heckleck said. "Let this be one of your first
introductions to the delights of the station and its ways of
keeping the peace among its citizens. Sometimes there are
quarrels between aliens and satisfaction can only be gained
by a fight."

"It's a sport?" I asked.

"No. It's not exactly a sport," Heckleck said. "This hocht
has been called because a Per who lives in the underguts is

demanding satisfaction from another Per who lives in the upper quarters who denied him entry to his sister's wedding because of his low grade status."

"So it's a duel?" I asked.

Heckleck cocked his head to his side as the nanites in him worked to help translate the English word I'd slipped in. Then he nodded.

"Yes, let's agree it's the same," he said.

"So I could have challenged you to a hocht over the plant?" I said.

He smiled, or rather what I knew now for his species passed as a smile.

"Interspecies fighting is forbidden."

"Why?" I asked.

"No two alien species are equally matched. One species always has an advantage. When two species fight, one always ends up dead. The hochts are meant to settle the minor disputes. After all, it's easier to clean up blood off a mat when the two contenders walk away alive."

It had surprised me to learn that most aliens carried knives, which was the leading cause of murder in space. Only the officers of the law like Tournour were allowed to keep two shot phase guns for absolute emergencies. Guns were too dangerous. Projectiles could cause hull ruptures. Phase guns could cause electrical problems. Both of those things meant death for all. Everyone followed this gun law on a spaceship or a space station.

The color of the dreary days changed when a solar flare or a meteor shower forced us all to evacuate to the station's emergency shelters. When a hocht happened or a ship arrived there was equal excitement. New people meant a

46

slight increase in activity. The few legitimate vendors on the station would raise their prices. The black market thrived. The dwellers in the underguts would rush to the docks to beg for day work. The prostitutes got paid enough to get them through until the next ship wandered this far away from the Central Systems.

After that first hocht, I grew to enjoy going to hochts when they were called every few months. I liked that there were postings that called out the charges that the instigator held against the opponent. The injustices were made public for all to see. I took a slight comfort in imagining myself calling a hocht on Brother Blue if he ever came back to the station. I liked the idea of everyone seeing his sins on display. But my argument with him was not minor, and I would not be soothed by a fight. I would not want him to walk away.

When Heckleck tired of gossip, he would sometimes talk to me about the old days. Of his youth. Of his planet. Of the places he'd seen. Of the enemies he'd made. Of those who he'd destroy when he could finally save enough to leave the station. He never talked about what had stranded him here, and I could read that it was a deep wound—likely as deep as mine. Betrayal and grief have a certain color no matter what the species is. Everyone in the underguts seemed to carry that color with them in their voice or walk or hunch.

If Heckleck was not around, I kept to myself, always plotting my way off the station. But eventually time dragged on and a few months turned into a year and here I was still on the Yertina Feray.

Despite my permanent numbness, there was a shard of hate in my heart that the inevitable march of time did not quell, and every day I was hit with the fact that everything was still strange. Still *alien*. The only thing that soothed me in any way was to look out of the largest windows at the planet Quint.

The arboretum was the only place with plant life, and it held the best view of the planet. No one ever seemed to gather there, as though looking at the greenery reminded them too much of the metal shell that surrounded them. But I liked it for the dirt and the strips of gel floor, soft to the feet, which mimicked standing on the surface of a planet.

Only Thado, the caretaker, ever spent as much time there as I did. After seeing that I did not come to do harm to the plant life, or to steal anything, he began to trust me. Often he would hand me a flash pad with a wish list of things he needed. Most of his harvest was presold at set times of the year. Legally, he was not allowed to sell anything from the arboretum. But anything that fell and was not harvested or matured out of season was fair game for him to trade with. He gifted the fruits and vegetables to me, and I made sure that they were gifted around the station. In return, the things that he needed seemed to find their way to him. I took a cut and no rules were breached. It was usually only a small basket, but fresh produce meant everything to space dwellers, regardless of if they lived in the underguts or above. Everyone traded for something fresh to eat.

I would go there, mostly to stare at Quint and at her continents and oceans until I swear I saw a life there. My imagination swelled at the thought of all of that land. I pictured a house built on what I supposed was a desert. I pictured the sky, filled with colors I could only pretend to know. I imagined cooling myself in the waters that I saw cut across the expanse. But in the end, I always had to return to my sorry state of being stuck on this station. And whenever my thoughts returned to the here and now, the loneliness was too much to bear. My reverie would end when the station rotated away, showing only space.

Then I would return to the underguts a little smaller. And I gladly suffered through any one of Heckleck's myriad conspiracy theories and reminiscences just to hear someone's voice.

"Why doesn't anyone live down there now?" I asked.

"No one can live down there," he said.

"But they did at one time," I said.

"Yes. But once everything got taken, miners moved on to the next place there was a rush for. And those that couldn't had the misfortune to be stuck here on the station. There were some who stayed and lived down there for a while. Hangers on. But even they eventually gave up when supplies became so short as to make living unlivable."

"But why not make a go of it?" I said. "Why not try to make the planet flourish?"

"There are many places that are not made for staying," Heckleck said. "They are too harsh, too hard, and too far away from whatever you call home. You don't root where you don't have to, unless you're unlucky."

It was true. One of the most remarkable things that I noticed about the Yertina Feray was the lack of children. No one wanted to breed in such a lost place. The few that were here were likely to never see their own home worlds. They grew up deprived of anything but frontier culture.

"But a person could live there," I said.

"You could. But the land is so depleted from the stripping of the planet that not much grows," he said. "Some insects and organisms. But even the animals left that place."

"Except alin flowers," I said. "On the Dren Line. I looked it up."

The flower was the only bright thing in my bin. I'd learned everything on how to care for it. It was a difficult task because the alin was not an easy plant to keep alive. I'd even been forced to give a cutting of it back to Tournour in order to get a bit of soil to help it thrive. I had been surprised to discover that it was a rare plant and had some interesting and potent medicinal uses, especially its pollen.

"Yes, but not enough of them to distill their pollen into any real use," Heckleck said. "That would be worth something."

I could see Heckleck calculating the value of an abundance of alin flowers and then sighing at the impossibility of it ever happening.

"If it were easy to settle on any planet and make it a home, then there would be more than Five Major Species," Heckleck said. "The map is always changing."

I liked when Heckleck said that. It was comforting. It was as though you could accidentally find yourself in the right place, if it was the right time. The Yertina Feray had been on the good side of the map once, and nothing meant that it wouldn't be again.

I put my hand on the metal of the floor and thought about Quint. The Yertina Feray, Quint, and I all had something in common. We'd been left behind.

"The Yertina Feray is lucky to be at a good crossroads in the known galaxy. It's a useful transfer point for light skips between the fringe of the Central Systems and the farthest Outer Rim systems. But other than that, we're a pretty useless place to be now," Heckleck said.

Which meant that there was a steady enough flow of people on the station for it to be safe. It would survive even in the leanest of times. I had heard tales of other space stations that were not so fortunate when the planets they surrounded had been stripped to nothing. Those stations had been abandoned, and the people on them had been left to die.

Heckleck rubbed his back wings together. When he did that and made a mournful sound, I had learned that it was the equivalent of a Human sigh. Whenever he talked about the politics and history of the known galaxy, he rubbed those wings a lot.

"It's so confusing. Humans aren't Minor because Earth wants to be left alone, and because I became a colonist to try to make us Minor, now I can't go home."

The rules of the galaxy had been made up long ago. The first worlds to travel and settle were the Major Species. Those Major Species fell in and out of power. They passed off power, keeping the center of the map rotating like a fiery ring of suns. They stretched their reach as far as they could. But new planets were always being discovered. New life. New civilizations.

"If you ask me, any species that is capable of space travel should be called Major," Heckleck said. "This Imperium will be the death of every Minor Species."

7

• •

Thado was pruning his plants and trees as I stared at Quint below.

I stepped onto the gel floor and closed my eyes, imagining for a moment that I was on a planet. The thing about the gel floor is that you had to adjust your sense of balance. That's what made it feel so real. Once balance was achieved, I stepped toward the window slowly, as though I were a ship on approach. I liked to trick my eyes and see the planet get larger. When I got close to the window, I slipped off my shoes and stepped right into the potted flower box, wiggling my toes in the dirt. *Dirt*. How it made memories of Earth rush back. My whole life had been made of dirt and now it was measured by the sheer lack of it. I was starving for dirt.

I put my hands up to the window, pressing my palms flat against it. It was thick—too thick to feel either the coldness of space or the warmth of the weak sun. I put my forehead on the window and opened my eyes. If I squinted just right, I could trick myself into thinking that I was falling freely through space, that I was tumbling toward that planet. It was the only way that I could ever feel free, even for one small moment, from my circumstances. It was the only moment where I remembered—for a flash—what it was like to be

Human and felt released from the anger that I had toward Brother Blue and what he'd done to me. He was out there. Somewhere. One day he would pay for it.

It was hard to think of what course of action I could take. I could not go back to Earth for help. I had no currency or connection to hitch rides with the Humans who roamed. Sometimes, I thought that my best strategy would be to go to one of the Children of Earth colonies first. But all of my attempts to communicate to the other Children of Earth colonies had been futile. Something was always in the way. Transmissions were interrupted by solar flares, or the relay was out of range, or there was just white noise.

I rested my head against the window, alone with my dark thoughts, trying to push them into space. As I entered my imaginary life, I heard a cough. At first I didn't turn around.

"I am supposed to arrest you," Tournour said. "It's forbidden to get so near the plants."

I said nothing. If he were going to arrest me, he would not have announced himself. I had been working mostly nights so I had not crossed paths with him in a while. Though we rarely spoke when we did meet, it always made me feel safer when I ran into Tournour on my errands. Often, he showed up at the end of a hallway or at the entrance to a hangar just when I was most scared. There he'd observe me, but not interfere.

I heard him rustle and move closer. Then I heard him unsnap his boots, and in the next moment he was standing with me in the plants.

"Interesting," he said. "It does feel nice."

I didn't have to answer. In my dealings with him, I'd learned that Tournour just liked to talk sometimes. Besides, if I said anything he might be obliged to haul me in. If I didn't speak, it could be as though I didn't exist.

We stood there for what seemed like hours, but was likely only a handful of minutes. Though he was looking at the planet with his eyes, I could feel that his antennae were turned toward me.

I settled back into being lost, looking out at the inky blackness and the beauty of the planet we orbited. Suddenly the black was cut by a glint. It was an object coming into view as it came around the planet. It flashed. It went from blue to orange. For a moment, my eyes tricked me and I thought that the object had come from the planet's surface.

"There's someone down there," I said excitedly, breaking the silence.

But that was impossible because I knew there was nothing down there anymore. Not even a colony. Any settlers had been moved to the Yertina Feray more than one hundred years ago.

I could feel Tournour's attention shift to the object, too. In unison, we both pressed closer to the window, as though that would make the object become clearer to us. It was a ship. It must have light skipped into the system on approach from the other side of the planet.

"What is that?" I said. It looked like no ship I'd ever seen.

"What we saw was an explosion. It's just been destroyed."

I followed his finger as it pointed to the object, now drifting closer in pieces.

"No, it can't be a ship, it's not moving, and it's floating. Like an asteroid."

"That's just debris. Look, there is a bigger ship."

Sure enough there was a bigger ship. The biggest I'd ever seen in my time on the Yertina Feray.

Tournour's body tensed, he released a scent.

I immediately felt a calm rush over me.

He clicked his communiquer on his wrist to check in with his superior, and I could hear a whispered set of orders being issued to him. Then he stepped out of the planter and began shaking the dirt off his feet. By the way that Tournour's mouth was set, I thought that he was angry. Perhaps angry at me. And then I saw the tremor in his hand. He wasn't angry. He was scared.

"What is it?" I said. I meant the ship, but I also wanted to know what scared him.

He looked up at me as he put on his boots.

"The Imperium has reached us."

I turned and looked back out the window. I could see the ship more clearly now. It was enormous. It was clearly some kind of warship. It had battle damage on it, and it was heading for the station. It didn't take long to see the Imperium banner on its side.

The Imperium had expanded and seized control, even all the way out here. Though we'd technically been under their jurisdiction since they'd dismantled the League of Worlds, no one thought that an Imperium warship would ever come this far.

I felt as though I should be more panicky than I was. Somehow the calm remained. I felt clearheaded. I thought about what needed to be done before that ship docked, and then I became overwhelmed with excitement. This could be good news for me. The Imperium actually arriving meant big changes in business and more opportunities for me to possibly make my exit. I could be closer to answers. For the first time in forever, my heart seemed light. But I could tell that Tournour did not feel that way, and I knew that Heckleck, with his myriad of conspiracy theories would not be happy with the Imperium's arrival either.

Tournour turned to leave me there, but stopped and looked back at me.

"Are you all right? How do you feel?" Tournour asked.

"Calm," I said.

"Of course you do," he said. He no longer looked scared.

I stepped out of the dirt but didn't bother to brush any of it off. I picked up my shoes and made my way to the lift.

I had only one thought. Find Heckleck and let him know.

The map was changing.

8

. . . .

The Yertina Feray had been invaded, but there were no explosions when the Imperium arrived. The only thing that got louder were the announcements that blasted all over the station intercom every hour upon the hour.

"Glorious citizens of the Imperium: We are here as friends. We are interested in peace and prosperity. We welcome an ongoing dialogue."

The dialogue, apparently, was not with the underguts. It took the Imperium days to even make their way down to the guts of the station. They were in dark green uniforms. They were aliens from all the Major Species and all the Minor Species who were closely collaborating with them. They came in with batons and knocked on everyone's bins.

"We are registering you for our records. Think of it as a census." The registration would begin right away.

A rumor spread that jobs could be had. One could get a quick exit pass to go to the Central Systems, now fully under Imperium occupation. They were looking for workers to work on planets with certain atmospheres and gravities. One could work in exchange for a ticket and travel pass off of the Yertina Feray and gain protection from the Imperium regardless of species.

I'd settle for any planet; especially if it got me moving toward finding Brother Blue or led me to one of the Human colonies. I wished that my mother and sister were out there, waiting for me.

"It's a war that does not feel like a war," Thado said when I snuck up to the arboretum for my fix of dirt.

"What does it mean?" I asked. "Are we free?"

"No," Thado said.

"I hear they are offering good hard work. We just need to sign up."

"They've made sure to try to tie us all even tighter to them," he said.

On my way out, he gave me a basket of fallen fruits and vegetables for those of us stuck in the underguts of the station. It was a big kindness, and I would not forget it.

I made my way back to the underguts where Heckleck was waiting for me. I told him of my plan.

"This is it! Isn't it wonderful we could be leaving soon!"

"Safer here. Collaborators who control the fringe of an empire are easier to manipulate than tyrants at the center," Heckleck said.

I didn't care if there were Minor Species collaborating with the Imperium. All I knew was that Brother Blue was out there and travel was denied to me as long as I remained poor and stuck as I was. Signing up for hard labor could at least get me moving. It was about a six-month contract with a promise of settlement permits when the contract was fulfilled.

Every Minor Species alien living in the underguts had their opinion. The more the aliens talked and passed along rumors, the more Heckleck rubbed away. He was more agitated lately. He spent hours in his bin, organizing and reorganizing his things.

As for me, I had a plan for myself. Heckleck had joined me and watched as I started packing my few pathetic things into a small bag.

He began rubbing his wings. His mournful song did not stop as he spoke.

"You're packing," Heckleck said. "Where are you going?"

"They're giving passes to go work places and eventual resettlement," I said. "And you know anywhere off of here—that's where I want to go. I'm going to get out of here."

"They're giving out death sentences," Heckleck said. "I've seen this before. Don't move until you know how everything has landed."

"They're offering work."

"Hard labor perhaps. Work that will kill you on planets that are unsuitable for your kind."

"I am strong. I am young."

"You should go in the other direction if you go anywhere," Heckleck said. "Go to the Outer Rim. Disappear."

I had always thought of Heckleck as endowed with an inner strength that I could depend on. But something out there, in the galaxy, frightened him enough that he kept himself here. The Yertina Feray was known, and there was a comfort in that. But beyond this station was where I needed to go if I were to ever have peace in my heart.

"I can't," I said. "There is something that I have to find out."

"Revenge is a good motivator, but it always disappoints in the end," Heckleck said. "Trust me. I tried it once."

He ever so slightly lifted his wing and revealed a deep discolored scar. It was a gash that looked as though it had nearly killed him. But here is where we differed. His scar made him stay—mine made me ache to leave.

There was a strange silence between us. Our friendship was ending. I would likely never see him again once I left. I knew that if I could help it, I would never set foot again on the Yertina Feray. I would find Brother Blue and make him pay for harming me and contributing to the death of my family. And then I would go to a colony and I would settle there as I had always planned.

I put my arm on Heckleck's appendage.

"Thank you for everything."

It seemed clumsy and not grateful enough, but it was the only thing I could say.

"The Imperium is corrupt. This station is also corrupt," Heckleck said. "We are but a buffer between the mad and the free. But it's safer here, or on the Rim, if you can get there. You should take my advice. Hide."

"No one, not even those that live on the Outer Rim, are undeclared," I said. "Everyone has taken a side."

"Well, I haven't," Heckleck said. "I'm on my side."

But I was excited by the possibility of change. Couldn't he see that? No, likely he couldn't. That was one of the troubles with some aliens, they couldn't interpret body language and social cues in other species. Heckleck failed at recognizing subtleties, which is why I was such an asset to him. One of the things that had helped me to survive was my ability to read aliens and mimic appropriately.

Still, it was nearly impossible to say goodbye.

"I suppose this is where we part, Heckleck," I said.

"I'm sorry to see you go," Heckleck said. "As my comrade in trade, I ask you one favor."

I looked at Heckleck. If he was cashing in a favor, then he was quite serious about what he was saying. Favors were valuable. And Heckleck never liked to owe anyone.

"Name it," I said.

We touched arms to seal the deal, as was the Hort way.

"Please don't help them find me if they come looking. They always round up Hort in the first rounds of exterminations."

"It's labor work, not death camps," I said.

"Regardless. It's our appearance that often offends so many species and we breed so quickly that new regimes like to cut down our numbers when they can. They excel in keeping us Hort a Minor Species."

"I promise," I said.

"Good luck to you then," Heckleck said. And then he disappeared down the corridor.

My heart was heavy as I turned to join the other aliens looking for a way out of here. The thought of being alone again triggered something deep inside of me. A panic that made me want to pull out all of my hair. I had to keep reminding myself that I was leaving, not the one being left. Once I mixed in with the rabble who usually waited at the docks begging for day jobs, I began to feel excited again. Here now we all waited on the line hoping to get chosen for job on a planet with a choice position in the galaxy.

Soon, I thought. *Soon*.

In just a short while I would find Brother Blue, and I would hurt him.

How I longed to set foot on a planet. I could feel myself nearly there. I tried to remember what a sun looked like in a sky.

"Next," an Imperium guard shouted.

"Human," I said.

The Imperium Guard looked up at me. She was about to enter me into the system to match me with an appropriate planet when Tournour stepped up. I wished Tournour would go busy himself with overseeing some other piece of business.

"This one is no good," he said. "You know how it is with these Humans. Weak immune systems. Poor stamina. The planets you're recruiting for here would kill her in a month."

If I could kill someone with my eyes, I would have killed him at that moment.

"I'm strong. I can work," I said, hoping to get the guard to pay attention to me and ignore Tournour. I wouldn't let my chance of getting off the station slip away so easily.

"If she were headed for a place like Nuvia, or Canlaghan, then I would say take her. On those planets she'd have enormous strength," said Tournour.

"Great," I said. "Send me to Nuvia or Canlaghan."

"We're not shipping there," the guard said.

Tournour was standing there, and I could not look at him or I would explode. I needed to remain calm in order to make sure that I was assigned to a ship out of here. He had the power to throw me into the brig if he saw fit, and that would ensure that I wouldn't leave.

"Well, I am fit to work," I said. "Your announcement said there was work for anybody."

"I didn't realize there were any of your kind this far out," the guard shook her head in disgust.

"She's our only one," Tournour said. His antennae were twitching from side to side, but he kept his eyes fixed on me.

"When I was running cargo in the core they kept hitching passage," the guard said. "They're never going anywhere, just always going. Do you have a particular interest in this one? I don't judge."

Tournour made a noise. The guard was Brahar. They were the species who had instigated the coup and led the Imperium with the other four Major Species. I knew that the Brahar and the Loor had no love for each other. They shared a solar system and had been each other's first contact and first alien enemies. The Loor and the Brahar made up the oldest of the Major Species and were the first to strike out and explore the stars.

"Well, Human, we are not taking your kind today," the guard said.

Then she waved me away. But I would not give up my spot. I stood in place, ignoring the complaints of those anxious aliens waiting behind me.

"That's not fair," I said.

"Why don't you come along with me, Tula," Tournour said. He took me by the elbow and made an attempt to lead me away.

"Stay out of my business, Tournour," I said shaking him off. I knew that if I stayed here now, he'd slap me with a fine or a night in the brig, but I didn't care.

"I would like to work," I said. "I'm a quick learner. And I'm stronger than he thinks."

The guard laughed.

"No doubt," she said. "I can see that you are feisty."

I wondered if I was supposed to bribe the guard. I slipped my hard saved currency chit onto the table.

The guard looked at the chit and then back at me. Then

she looked at Tournour who shook his head at her. It was clear that my bribe had been trumped.

"Consider yourself lucky that I don't accept your volunteering," the guard said, waving me back to the living space. "Move along."

I took back my currency chit.

Tournour was close on my heels, as though he were ensuring that I actually went back to the underguts and didn't try to steal back and get through with another guard. When we were alone in a passageway I turned on him. It took every ounce in me to not punch him.

"Why?" I said. "Why did you block me from leaving?"

"We take care of our people here, even of a species like yours," he said.

"My affairs are none of your business," I said. "I am not one of your people."

He looked surprised.

"You are a citizen of the Yertina Feray," he said.

"I'm not! I don't want to be here! I want to get off of this station and move on with my life!"

"I'm sorry that you feel that way," he said.

"That's not good enough," I said.

"It's illegal to disobey a constable's orders," he said. "You'll have to come with me."

In all the time that I had been on the Yertina Feray, I'd done plenty of questionable things that Tournour knew about. By far my tantrum was the mildest of my infractions. So I was a bit in disbelief that he was actually hauling me in. I knew that the more I argued, the worse my sentence would be. I bit my tongue and followed him.

"Troublemaker?" his superior said.

"Disturbing the peace," Tournour said and put me in the brig. It was clean and empty.

"Humans," his superior said.

They kept me there for three days. When I was finally free, the Imperium ships and troops were gone.

I went to reclaim my bin and put away my things. The underguts were practically empty. I knew not to bother looking for Heckleck, but before I went to sleep, I took a walk around the now quiet living area. Those who had not been recruited were looting the now abandoned living spaces. Some were moving into and taking over the empty larger bins.

I took nothing. But I did note who looted and who didn't. I made a mental note to tell Heckleck that I would not deal with them.

After a few days of wandering the station, which before seemed empty but was now practically soulless, it became clear that those Minor Species who were considered undesirables were gone. And none of the Minor Species whose planets were known to be collaborating with the Imperium had been taken for hard labor. I had never concerned myself with who or what was running things, but it didn't take much observing to know that what the Imperium were doing was best for some but not for all. The Imperium had established a hierarchy of which species were not civilized enough to their mind to merit status.

With Heckleck in hiding, and the station so empty, my thoughts turned to my mother and Bitty. I missed them and hated that they were dead. I realized that even though being stuck on the Yertina Feray felt like a kind of hell, that I had been lucky to be stranded here and to be alive. That was already more than my mother and Bitty would ever have.

Sometimes I dreamt they were alive and in pain and calling

to me. When I awoke, my resolve to avenge them doubled. It was the only way I could answer their cries.

Somehow I knew that Heckleck had been right to hide and that I had been spared, and it was due to Tournour's intervention.

I resented that it was time to tuck into small places and keep a low profile.

Now I would owe Tournour another favor that I couldn't repay not only because the favor had been too big but because he had left with the Imperium ships.

The Imperium wanted a sympathetic infrastructure running all of the planets and stations under their jurisdiction, so there was a shift of personnel as the old planetary delegates that ran the station under the League of Worlds were removed and the Yertina Feray awaited Imperium-installed delegates to run the station. For now, except for the gutter dwellers, some low-ranking aliens to keep the station up and running, a few of the Imperium Guard, and those who had made a home here, the Yertina Feray was a ghost town. What was surprising was that Tournour, who was not in charge of anything, had been called to leave.

Since there was no infrastructure to accommodate them during this time, most ships that approached the station were turned away from docking. Travel, which was already tightly restricted, became nearly impossible. Word came down that from now on in order to leave the station or to travel in Imperium space, a travel pass was required. Even currency would not get you anywhere without a pass. Everyone was stuck. The station seemed to be in hibernation.

It was during this quiet time that Heckleck reemerged, knocking on my bin as though he had never been away.

There were rumblings in the underguts and above levels about what was going on but no certainty, and it infused a diet of steady fear in everyone. I was learning that uncertainty was bad for business. People were more conservative when they were afraid, and hungry. Even the most civilized started to become a little feral. I could see that Heckleck's and my way of living could not survive an empty station.

"Shall we go gather ourselves a meal from the arboretum? Thado is sure to have too many edibles on his hands," Heckleck said.

I nodded. I knew better than to ask where he'd been as we walked to the arboretum.

We made our way up level by level. Every door was closed. Every store was shuttered. Even the cleaning bots were quiet and in their charge stations. It was normal for many doors and quarters to be boarded up and in disarray, but even this was unnerving. If I didn't know for certain that there were at least two hundred people on the station, I would be certain that we were alone.

"It's quiet. Even Tournour's gone. It's a little lawless right now," I said as I picked through the basket of vegetables that Thado had set out for us.

"Someone will be back to keep us all in order," Heckleck said. "The Imperium will place their puppet administrators here to run the Yertina Feray."

I remembered the stories I'd heard about the dead and forgotten space stations left to die.

"Do you think we'll be forgotten?" I asked Heckleck and Thado. When I spoke the words, my tongue felt thick, and things seemed unreal.

"We've always been forgotten and still managed to exist.

Things will return. They always do," Thado said. He passed us each a glass of pressed juice he had prepared.

"I never pegged you as a hopeful one, Thado," I said.

"I'm not hopeful, I'm experienced," he said. With so few on the station, we were all eating well from the arboretum. The situation had its tiny perks after all.

"But no one has returned yet," I said. It had been over a month.

"They will come," Thado said. "You will see."

Thado had calmed me before when he'd found me in those first few months, trembling in the arboretum, shaking for reasons I couldn't understand. His voice was mellow and low, and I would focus on it and the panic would subside.

"We're far away but not as far as some, and if the Imperium wants to expand, we're strategic," Heckleck said. "We're still useful as a light skip point."

I had to take Heckleck and Thado's words on this. They were more universal than I was in these matters.

"The Imperium wants control of its rabble, and even if it doesn't have enough of a military force to occupy every planet outside of the Central Systems, the Imperium knows that if the fringes are left to the fringe, rebellions could breed like simple life forms that take over if not kept in check," Thado said.

Heckleck stretched his little wings out and began to thrum.

"The people that they place here will keep the rabble from behaving in a manner that is unsuitable to Imperium plans," Heckleck said. "Never underestimate the power of a lowly bacteria to evolve and thrive."

"It's good to know that we still have our uses," I said.

"But it will be a chore to learn anew who is bribable when they return," Heckleck said.

"Whatever do you mean?" Thado said, feigning surprise. After all, he'd always been in our pocket, even though he worked for the station. We laughed. It was a light moment, and I was thankful for it.

• •

After getting his bearings, Heckleck could see how quiet the station had become. It irritated him that there was almost nothing to do.

"So difficult getting things done with such a shortage of lowlifes and high-placed officials on the station," Heckleck said.

The lack of things to do had made me depressed. I was back at square one. With the travel restrictions and the changing of the currency values, everything I had worked for before the Imperium arrived was now worthless. Heckleck sensed my misery.

"Do you know what the best thing to do is when a place is empty?" Heckleck asked.

"No," I said.

"Explore," Heckleck said. "Come, let me show you what I've found while I was in hiding."

He took me up to sections of the station that I'd never seen before. He showed me secret spots for hiding things. We went into the deep altars of temples where species worshipped no longer. Into the storage lockers of those who left at the end of the mining boom, certain that they would be back to gather their things. Into the vents of air supplies to sections that no longer needed specialized atmospheres or gravities. The sheer abundance of sections hinted at the vastness of the number of Minor Species. I felt that despite how many aliens I had seen during my time on the Yertina Feray, I had barely interacted with the galaxy at all.

Heckleck and I crawled in crawl spaces to scoot around high above the closed off sectors, likely used when maintenance was necessary in those places, but now quite forgotten. We had a bird's-eye view of everything.

One space we stumbled into was a warehouse full of machines that looked like insects.

"What are they?" I asked.

"Miners," Heckleck said.

They were frightening—rows and rows of faceless mining robots.

We walked, picking our way between them, these miners from a forgotten past that had ravaged and depleted the world below.

"Do they work?" I asked.

Heckleck picked up one of their heads from the ground.

"No."

"They sort of look like you," I said.

"My dear girl, just because they are insect-like does not mean that we are similar."

But they did look like the Hort: the way their legs and arms were folded in an insect-like way, the coppery color of their metal, their pinched faces and the large eyes. The only thing they were missing was tiny vestigial wings on their backs.

"They don't even have faces," Heckleck said.

"I don't mean to insult you," I said.

Heckleck began to flip switches and slide his appendage

on the panel of a computer terminal. But nothing happened. The rows of robots remained still.

"See. Useless," he said. "We can sell the metal, bit by bit. Galactic expansion always needs metal."

But I heard a hum to my right.

"Do you hear that?" I asked. I followed the sound, weaving through the rows of robots until I was standing in front of one robot with its lights on, but nothing else.

Heckleck turned the power off and the lights on the robot went dim.

"Not this one," I said. I took a marking device from my pocket and I drew a face on the one that had lit up. "This one is mine."

"Suit yourself," Heckleck said. "You do attach yourself to such strange things."

We had a good haul from the closed up places we'd discovered. It was useless now, with barely anyone to barter with, but would come in handy bit by bit later. It wasn't looting if you took items that had been abandoned for over a century. That was fair game. It surprised me what valuables people had left behind in the sections that had been closed for years.

"Why haven't you ever gone for this stuff before?" I asked.

"Because there were always eyes watching everything. Now, the station is blind. For these few months, we are free."

When we were back in the underguts with our finds, Heckleck offered me the last of the maggot-like delicacies of his planet that he'd recently procured. I ate them with relish. I had developed a taste for them. They tasted like life to me.

"It's strange, all these things we've taken from those who are likely long dead," I said.

"The dead are useful to our business," Heckleck said.

"They are not useful at all," I said. "They are dead."

"That is what you think. But the dead, they have ghosts. Ghosts are very useful for haunting. Never forget the dead, Tula. They have their function. They sometimes speak at the most useful or inopportune times."

I thought about my mother and sister. I could not imagine that they would be useful for anything. They were dead. Nothing that they had to say could ever help me from beyond the grave now. Their time for helpful words was done.

It was when I thought of them that the parts inside of me that used to feel hardened the most.

"I miss my family," I said. "I wish Brother Blue had died with the colonists."

When I thought of my mother and her trust in Brother Blue, I became angry. I was angry at him, but I was angrier at her. Why did she trust me with him? Why couldn't she see that he was dangerous? Why did she blindly take my sister onto the *Prairie Rose* without me? Why did she have to die? Even if I did manage to avenge them, they would still be dead, and they would still be silent. It was the silence that hurt me the most.

I remembered how all of the colonists looked at Brother Blue as though he were a God. Even I did. After assisting him, however, I remembered feeling as though I were faking my fervor. I began to see a normal man who looked to be full of shadows. But I could not place my finger on what was off.

I only knew that he always lit up when he said that the galaxy and its core were full of possibilities of richness beyond dreams. That was the only time that he ever seemed to be telling the truth. I was certain that it was true. There was something to be won out in that vastness.

• •

Soon enough, the station slowly began to wake up as the first ship finally docked. The new, even when unknown, is infectious in its possibilities. I found Heckleck in his bin, sorting his stock of salts.

"I'm going to find out what's going on," I said.

"Careful, we'll have to work hard to see who is bribable," Heckleck said.

"Maybe it'll be more interesting," I said. "Maybe I'll find another way off of here."

Heckleck just rubbed his wings together.

I made my way over to the docking bays. I could see the new security force helping to move the transition of new people as they arrived. I didn't recognize any of them as the new members of station security until they moved into the light. It was Tournour.

I had not expected him to be there. I had not expected to ever see him again. It surprised me that he had been sent back. Part of me wanted to march right up to him and yell at him again for keeping me on the station when I could have been gone months ago and on my way to revenge. But the change in mood on the station kept me in check. I hung back and I watched as some of the other new delegates streamed off the arriving ships. I noticed only the ones in charge spoke. They had been gifted a high-ranking position, even if it was in the backwater of space. They knew they had power. But it was not them that I watched. They were useless to me. Heckleck had advised me to look at the ones that were arriving to be new citizens of the station, the ones with the lower clerical-type jobs. They looked as though they all wanted to be as invisible as possible. They would be desperate. They would be the people to approach. They were the aliens who would trade for favors. But I could not observe them as thoroughly as I wanted to because my eyes kept going back to Tournour as he stood there organizing the whole arrival.

He couldn't see me from where he was. I knew that it would be better to stop staring and to get out of there as quickly as possible in case he caught me and I did something that got me into more trouble with him. Besides, by the Imperium threads Tournour was wearing, it was clear he was working with them. There was no mistaking his alliance. I felt my heart, which had almost jumped when I saw his familiar face, snap shut. Heckleck had always told me it was silly to think of anyone in power as an ally. Even if their actions seemed to indicate a bond, they would always betray you in the end. The higher up they were, Heckleck always said, the more confusing their actions could be.

I made my way back down to the underguts.

"Well, what shall I give you for the information?" Heckleck asked.

He knew full well that he had to give me nothing.

"You don't owe me anything," I said.

"Then I haven't taught you well," he said.

"All right," I said, pointing to the fattest fruit in his bowl. "I want the fattest, juiciest one. The one I know you're saving for last."

"That is a high price," he said. He pretended to consider my offer. Then he plucked it from the bowl and gave it to me.

"Tournour is back," I said. "I thought we'd never see him again."

"He must have done something terribly wrong to be exiled here," Heckleck said. "On second thought, perhaps if he's been disgraced there is hope."

"He's not disgraced. He was helping to organize the transition," I said.

"That's the trouble with officers of the law," Heckleck said. "They are always on the wrong side."

"Unless you can buy them," I said.

"I've been trying to buy Tournour for years," Heckleck said. "Terribly stubborn Loor."

• •

The first time I saw Tournour again was at the game tables at Kitsch Rutsok's. He had just gotten off duty. I went up to him as he sat enjoying a drink of jert juice with a female of his species. I thought he looked different. Somehow terrible and quite unlike his old self, and it was more than just his new uniform.

"Tournour," I said.

He seemed surprised that I would approach him.

I wanted to see up close if he was really changed. I couldn't say that it was nice to see him. He had chips in his hand. I'd never known him to play the games of chance before. He had never even wagered on a hocht. But here he was, placing bad bet after bad bet. He ignored me, and instead pawed the Loor female he was with. He was laughing, but it sounded forced. I had been reading Tournour my entire time on the station, and he did not seem to be having as much fun as he was pretending to.

And then there were his antennae, they were not pointed

at the female, they were pointed away. They were pointed at me. I was keenly aware of them, like they were an extra set of eyes watching me.

I was being ignored, and I saw that it was useless to pursue any kind of conversation with him.

I circled back to exit.

Tournour had followed me.

He was tall, powerful, and, now that I was standing this close to him, threatening. I knew that no one would protect me in the bar if he went after me. He leaned in close. I was surprised at how sweet he smelled.

"I remember the stories of when your people first came," Tournour said. "My grandfather met a few of your firsts. So primitive were you Humans when you arrived on your generational ships. People who had forgotten what a planet felt like because they were ship-born."

Earth's first true pioneers were those Humans who first traveled to the stars on generational ships. Everyone on Earth claimed to have someone who had gone on one of those generational ships. It was romantic to think that you had family in the stars.

My grandmother, who couldn't even remember her own name or what she had for breakfast, would talk fondly about the day that the first light skip ships piloted by aliens had arrived carrying Humans who had hitched a ride home.

But those Humans came back to a different Earth than the overcrowded one that they had left. They were not welcome, and so they and theirs were forced back to wander the stars.

Tournour had his intense gaze fixed on me, as though he wanted me to say something.

"Aren't all of us who live on the station a bit like that?" I said. "It's been a long time since I've set foot on a planet. I've forgotten what it's like, too."

"It's pleasant," Tournour said. "Sunlight is pleasant. The warmth of it. We have the same kind of star, you and I. Did you know that?"

I shook my head no.

"Such similar homes," he said.

He said it as though I was meant to understand something. But I didn't.

"A sun warms in a way that a lamp can't. Or maybe it's the birds," he said.

"So your trip back home was good?" I asked.

Tournour grimaced. A shadow passed over his face as though he were going to say something but then stopped himself.

"I'm back and in charge. They've promoted me," he said. "That's how it went."

I had my answer. He could not be bought.

9

New administrators began to take the place of the old. Aliens boasted of the changes that would be made with the fresh start. Shops reopened. Goods arrived. The ships returned—a few at first—and then more. Things were mostly back to the way they were. I had been on the Yertina Feray for three earth years.

And then one day they came.

I was not prepared for them. I hadn't heard about their ship arriving. I'd been deep in a series of trades and that sometimes took hours before being resolved.

It was late in the day, and I'd missed the gutter meal call, so I decided to treat myself to a luxury dish at Kitsch Rutsok's bar. There were three of them. They showed up in a group on their way to get food.

Humans.

Once I saw them I could not stop staring. I had forgotten the sizes and shapes of my species. I'd forgotten the differences between males and females. The different colors of skin, hair, and eyes.

They took a table and sat down; they looked out of place among the aliens that made up the fabric of my day-to-day life. When I looked closer, I realized they looked my age, about seventeen or eighteen. Stranger still, they were all wearing green Imperium uniforms. As far as I knew, Earth was still undeclared. They weren't part of a Children of Earth colony ship. They must be a part of the Humans that still roamed the stars. It was clear that they had nanites as they weren't wearing breathing masks or having trouble communicating. They probably had taken up the offer by the Imperium on labor work. I was jealous, but comforted by the thought that they'd likely be on their way soon.

Instead of eating protein paks, they ordered real food, which meant this week they were eating Per food, which had recently arrived on a Per ship. Very salty. Their faces betrayed nothing of the extreme taste. They looked down, trying to avoid the sneers of the species around them. They were frightened, that much was clear. Seeing Human fear made me feel fearful for them. It was as though seeing it on a Human face made me understand it within myself. Fear was not something that I liked when it bubbled up to the surface.

At last one of them looked up and finally noticed me. It was one of the young men. His dark eyes caught mine, and he looked surprised, as though he had not expected to see another Human here on the Yertina Feray. I wanted to look away but I could not. He tapped the boy and girl sitting next to him who looked over at me as well. Then they all stopped eating and stared. The first young man, the darker of the two boys, lifted his hand up and waved.

My heart raced. *Hello. Hello Human. Hello.*

Then my chest tightened. And an ache sprung up inside of me. Memories of my family flooded my mind. My throat constricted, and I thought I was ill, but then I remembered that it was what it used to feel like before I tried not to cry. I hadn't cried in so long, I didn't think I remembered how. Yet, the feeling persisted. I coughed, as though that would help dislodge the tightness. It didn't. I drank a glass of recycled water and as I swallowed I pushed the feeling aside. When the glass was drained, I tore my eyes away from the group and got up. I knew they were watching me as I left. I would not go to them. The last time I'd seen Humans, I had been betrayed. I couldn't be certain that these Humans were any different.

10

· ·

They were still onboard. These Humans didn't act as though they were leaving; they looked as though they were settling in. Most passers through stayed on their ships, but the first thing that these Humans did after they arrived was to go straight to the luxe accommodations and settle into an empty luxe suite. They created a lot of noise. They expected things. They tried to cheat merchants in not-so-clever ways. It was as though they felt that they were entitled to special deals or privileges and they behaved exactly in the way that made other species despise them. Was it Human nature? I recognized nothing of myself in them on that front. It had taken me such a long time to be accepted among the other aliens, to have my own place in the ladder of things. I was afraid they would undo my work.

While a part of me felt I should go to them, help them to get some basic needs, I could not move. It was as though a wall had been constructed around me that would not fall no matter how hard my humanity tried to scale it. I did not feel like I was one of them.

I wondered how it was possible to feel two things at the exact same time. I wanted to help them and myself, and yet I also wanted to stay away from them. Was it something that I had forgotten about being Human? This duality of mind? Of knowing one thing in your head, of having a plan of how to accomplish your own goals, follow your own agenda, but also having a feeling that opposed it in your heart? It was maddening. It muddied my ability to think properly.

"Why are they moving in?" I asked Heckleck. "Why aren't they staying on their ship?"

The truth was that seeing other Humans made me feel anxious. I knew how to act when I was the only Human on the Yertina Feray. I did not know how to when I was one of a few.

"The rumor is their ship exploded and they were rescued in escape pods by some Per," Heckleck said. "We were the closest stop."

I put my hand up. I did not want to know any more about them. They would surely be on their way soon. There was no reason for them to stay here.

I tried to steer clear of them on my rounds, but I had to pass by their quarters, which were located on a main crossing and therefore unavoidable. Whenever I did, I couldn't help but notice that they were always playing music. That was something that I had forgotten about, how much music there used to be in my life when I lived on Earth. I never stopped when I passed by their dwelling, but today it was a song that I remembered.

I could almost catch my youth when the notes drifted over to me, as though it was a stray thread of a memory that I could pull on. The melody streamed out and hit me right in the heart and then twisted. It was so familiar, and it brought back such a vivid memory that I had to catch my breath.

I closed my eyes.

I could remember standing on the porch of my house looking out over the field. My father was on the swing next to me, drinking a beer. It was hot. My sister, Bitty, played with the hose as Mother weeded the vegetable garden. The smell of Grandmother's cooking wafted out from inside. My father turned up the volume on the music player and began to sing along.

This was before my mother had started taking the Children of Earth pamphlets home and leaving them on the table for my father to find. Before she started disliking everything in our life on Earth. Before I noticed that things on Earth weren't how I saw them. *Before.*

In that moment, listening to the tune as it embraced me, I could remember what being happy felt like at the remembrance of things past that I had long ago pushed down and forgotten.

What were the words to that song again?

I leaned forward trying to catch the lyrics but they were too faint to hear. They touched the edge of my brain and snuck in, looking for a pathway to unlock the old memory. I moved my lips as though moving them would somehow make me know the words. But no matter how hard I tried to access it, I could not remember them.

And then I heard a snatch of another voice singing, not from the music recording, but from one of the Humans, the blond one. He had stepped outside of the quarters and was singing to himself. His voice was melodic, bright, and round. There was something about hearing a person sing that was so primal. The notes made their way down to the very bones of me. I stepped back, pressing myself into the shadows trying to blend in, not wanting to be caught. But I stumbled. And suddenly there he was catching my elbow, helping me up from the ground.

"You all right?" he asked.

I nodded.

He opened his mouth again as though to further the conversation. Or perhaps his lips were forming a smile. Smiling in return would be an invitation to more, and I didn't want to know anything except the name of the song. I was too proud to ask for that information. I pulled my jacket down and went on my way.

"Wait," he said.

I liked the sound of his voice. Even more when he spoke than when he sang. I liked the familiar common tongue we shared.

He picked up the small bag of tools that I'd dropped. I hadn't noticed that they'd fallen, and it would have cost me a few days to replace them. He'd unknowingly done me a favor. I nodded in thanks, but still did not speak.

If they were staying on the station, I still wasn't ready to talk to them. I wasn't sure that I wanted to associate with them. They were rude and loud and made me embarrassed to be a Human. No. It was more than that. They made me feel as though I were skinless, and that hurt.

It's all right, I thought. *Just because we're the same species didn't mean that we had to be friends.*

11

· ·

I made my way to the arboretum. The music had stung me, and when I was upset, the arboretum was the only place that calmed me. Besides, Thado owed me a favor and he had at least one bale of Machi leaf that I needed.

Thado was on a ladder picking some blue trests that had ripened and looked ready to eat. I watched him for a minute; sometimes I imagined that he was like a glorious sea creature, but then inevitably my eyes always drifted to the window, reminding me that I was far away from any ocean. Quint looked angry to me today. Right now the largest ocean on its surface was facing us. I knew it was windy season. Winds were whipping over parts of the planet at high speeds. I wondered what it sounded like. I missed wind. I watched until the Dren Line came into view.

"Here," Thado said, and as I turned he threw me a trest, my favorite alien fruit, which I caught and began eating. The juice was sweet and delicious.

"What can I do for you, Tula?" Thado asked.

"Machi leaf," I said.

He shook his head.

"It's not doing well right now. Some pest someone brought onboard is eating it."

"One bale."

"It will be a skinny bale," Thado said.

"Just make it look pretty," I said.

Thado nodded, meaning that I would get my bale. He descended the ladder in his elegant way and then handed me two baskets of trests.

• •

I had dropped off the first basket with a merchant who had traded me some working power packs when Tournour and his guards cornered me.

"Tula," Tournour said, taking one of the trests from the baskets and eating it. "Your hair looks shorter."

I knew that he hadn't caught up with me to talk about my hair. I ignored him. It was still best to remain quiet until he revealed what his real motive was.

"Have you seen them?" he finally asked.

"Seen who?" I asked. But I knew whom he meant. The Humans.

He smiled. He knew I was lying. He waited for me to speak. We were each waiting for the other to tip their hand. With his new position as chief constable he did not make as many rounds anymore, so we'd rarely spoken. There was a silence between us. But the quiet that stretched from me to him spoke volumes.

It was telling me that he was concerned for me. And it was telling him that he had a right to be concerned. He knew I was rattled. With Tournour there were always multiple layers of meaning between the words and the pauses.

"Just because I'm Human doesn't mean that I know every Human," I said.

"Of course not," he said.

"If you have questions about them, go ask them," I said.

"I've interviewed them already," he said. "That is my job."

He waited for me to ask what he knew. I wouldn't bite. He knew then that I knew nothing.

"They are from Earth. Their ship was destroyed in an explosion," he said. "And they are part of the Earth Imperium Alliance."

That surprised me. It meant that the Imperium had stretched its reach even further than the usual borders that shifted hands when power changed. It meant that Earth had changed its position on everything. Perhaps it meant that I could return there with time and currency. The map could be changing dramatically for me.

"They ran into trouble," he continued. "But they don't seem as though *they* are trouble."

"Good to know," I said.

"They're planning on leaving soon," he said. "They're just passing through. They're waiting for new travel passes from the Imperium. Then they'll get new orders."

"None of my business," I said.

I closed my eyes and tried to calm my wildly beating heart. Tournour stood there saying nothing. It bothered me that he was watching me as I tried to sort out my feelings. Sometimes I felt he could see into me in a way that no one else ever had. It was not pleasant. I wanted my dark insides to remain hidden. I wanted to be left alone.

I would risk a night in the brig to make him go away.

"Are you hauling me in or are we done?"

Tournour stared at me for a bit longer, likely trying to see if he could decipher what I was thinking. I kept my face as neutral as possible.

He took four more trests from the basket.

"Now we're done," he said, and then left me to go on his way.

12

. . . .

I wound my way up to the Ministry of Colonies and
Travel and planted a voucher for exotic girls at Kitsch Rutsok's on the desk of the alien in charge, Disanter, who knew
me well. I had been in so often trying to reach the Children
of Earth colonies since he'd told me about the fate of the
Prairie Rose, always to no avail.

"Tula Bane, I know what you want. The colony at Killick
has been on auto reply for three months. And the colony at
Andra reports it is still only responding to other Children
of Earth colonies unless there is an emergency," Disanter
said.

I couldn't understand why the colonies were so impossible to reach. When I first gathered enough currency, I had
tried to reach the other Children of Earth colonies hoping
that they would change their policies and take any Human
who wanted to settle. I used a fake name since I was afraid
of Brother Blue. But in the end it didn't seem to matter
who I was, they never answered. When I got through once to
Gelen, they had sent a message back saying they were a
closed colony. These days, I did not send messages when I
went to the Ministry of Colonies and Travel, rather I listened for chatter. I listened for the movements of Brother

Blue, but his whereabouts seemed to always be hidden from me.

I had long ago given up on contacting Earth. But now I wanted to know a little bit more about what was happening in my home section of the galaxy. Clearly Earth had joined the Imperium, and I did not know if they had joined willingly or if the Imperium had invaded.

"I want to listen to Earth chatter," I said.

His two mouths made surprised-looking Os and hummed an even tone. Disanter loved a change in routine.

I watched as he dialed in the coordinates for Earth and made a hail.

"It is interesting to note that they are using an Imperium channel now," Disanter said.

I could tell that he wanted to grab the voucher, but he restrained himself. He knew if he took his time, he could get bigger favors from me.

"What was the last transmission sent to or from Earth?" I asked.

It was not so easy to get immediate answers when trying to communicate in space. A message could take hours, and to some places even a day. And I was not the first to complain about the Yertina Feray's unbearably slow and outdated communication arrays. But if I could read those transmissions from the Humans on the station, or decode some Earth chatter, I would know a lot more right away.

"That's private information, and I am bound by the galactic communiquer laws to not divulge the any transmissions by private parties," said Disanter.

"I know that, and you know that, but perhaps you have a sudden urge to go get yourself a warm liquid drink of your choice. Surely, leaving your office for a few minutes is not a crime."

"No," he said. "It's not a crime."

He got up and took the voucher with him.

"Aren't you forgetting something?" I said before he reached the door.

He hadn't given me the pass code. He was trying to steal from me.

He laughed in a double harmony.

"How silly of me."

"Just because I'm being obvious with what I want doesn't mean that I've turned stupid," I said.

"Of course not," he said.

"That voucher is no good unless I send word to Kitsch Rutsok, and I won't send word unless I get what I came for."

"Of course," he came back to the desk and entered a long set of numbers and characters on the datapad. I picked up his communiquer and called Kitsch's to authorize the voucher. When the alien left the room, I got to work.

The chatter seemed to confirm Earth had joined the Imperium for its protection and Earth Gov had been re- placed by the Earth Imperium Alliance, but some of Earth Gov was still fighting for its old isolationist stance. There were ten messages to and from Earth regarding the Humans on the Yertina Feray. There was only one response. No matter how many times they had tried to reach Earth and beg for instructions and help, Earth had only one reply.

"Treason. Denied."

They had turned their pleas to the Human representative of the Earth Imperium Alliance on Bessen. They were now trying to appeal directly to the Imperium for help. So far they had no answer.

I cleared my tracks and exited the office.

They'd been burned. The Humans had been burned from going back to Earth just like me.

13

. . . .

Now armed with more information, I began to
observe the Humans with interest. What at first seemed ar-
rogant to me, now looked like desperation. I still kept my
distance, but the Yertina Feray was only so big and I could
not avoid them forever. That I would run into them was inevitable. And I had many questions.

I could not deny it. They had upended me.

After my visit to the Ministry of Colonies and Travel, it
didn't take long for our paths to cross.

I was standing in the makeshift market with Heckleck
when the Humans arrived on the other side of the square.
The girl went to the stands and began looking at some lace. I
had already looked at the lace; it was beautiful, but overpriced.
I could have easily traded it for a good favor but I made a
point to never buy anything at the market. I just liked to see
what people thought their wares were worth. If there was
one thing I had learned from Heckleck it was that in public,
things were worth more than in private. And that public price
was useful information to know.

"Straight for something useless," Heckleck said. "That's
good information for you to know."

As much as Heckleck knew me, and liked me despite
my being Human, he still harbored some hostility toward

Humans. Perhaps he was more sensitive than I ever gave him credit for and had noticed how preoccupied I was since they'd arrived. Perhaps his sharp words about them were to offer me protection and comfort.

I patted Heckleck's appendage.

"Good eye," I said. "I owe you one."

Although, really I didn't owe him anything for such a small observation, but it was our way and so I played along.

I moved on to the food stands and haggled myself a free graffa cake. I was licking the sticky sweetness off of my fingers.

"Oh, well, I'll take a small corner of your graffa cake then."

I handed him the last of the graffa cake, and he tore off a piece of it. And then tore that piece in half until he had not much more than a crumb.

"There, that should do," he said.

I smiled at him and turned away, as I was more interested in looking at the girl as she weaved her way through the stands. I noticed that she did not buy anything, but she fingered many items. She picked things up and then put them down, as though she were marking them.

She was raven-haired. I didn't remember ever seeing hair that blue-black when I was on Earth. It seemed fake somehow. Her features and skin looked as though she had been shaken in a bag of every kind of Human being. I noticed that she had curls and curves. She seemed more feminine than I remembered a girl being. I wondered how I compared. Then I pushed that thought aside. I didn't care.

The girl put down the glassware she was handling when the young man with dark hair joined her. The girl's attitude changed. She smiled and touched the boy playfully. The boy put his arm around the girl's waist, and they moved into the crowd.

As I began to make my way out of the market, I was approached.

It was the Human girl. She'd waited until I was alone.

"This is silly," the girl said. "We can't just ignore each other."

I brushed her off and moved up to the seats. But she was persistent and followed me.

"My name is Els Ribinder," she said. And then she smiled. Her teeth were whiter than I remembered teeth being. It was nice to see a Human smile. So many things looked like smiles but weren't. Sometimes, to feel genuine kindness again, I would stare into a mirror and smile at myself, just to remember what one looked like. But here was a real smile, right in front of me. Up close.

It irritated me that she had told me her name. It meant that they would not be just "the Humans," now.

"I hear you can get things," Els said.

"There are things here," I said, indicating the makeshift market.

"Yes, but not what I want," Els said. "Besides, the prices here are steep."

I observed as Els tilted her head to the side. She twisted a piece of hair. She gazed underneath her eyelashes. I remembered Bitty doing the same thing to get a piece of chocolate, or a toy that she wanted from the store. I remembered that it always worked on our parents. But whenever I tried, it failed.

Still, I tilted my head to mirror Els's.

"Depends on what it is," I said.

"Lotion," Els said. "This space station air is so much harsher than our ship was. My skin is about as dry as a lizard."

"Lizard," I said, and then laughed. "I'd forgotten about lizards."

"We're far from Earth now," she said, laughing with me.

It was those little details, that when remembered, delighted me. Lizards, small reptiles that used to scurry under the rocks near my house. I liked them better than snakes, whose slithering always scared me.

And lotion. I remembered my mother's lotion. It smelled like magnolias. My mother would put it on after she showered. It was a luxury. But the dry desert heat demanded such luxuries. On occasion my mother would let Bitty and me put a little bit on our hands. My mother had shipped a crate of magnolia lotion with her on the *Prairie Rose*. I closed my eyes. I could not remember what a magnolia looked like. It was getting harder and harder to remember what flora and fauna looked like from back home. All I could picture were the strange otherworldly plants in the arboretum.

As Els spoke, I could almost remember what my mother's voice sounded like. They had a similar lilt.

There is nothing here anymore. Better to go to the stars.

"It will cost you," I said.

"I don't have that much currency," Els said. "What will it cost?"

"I'll take a thing or a favor."

Els looked at me and smiled. Then she pulled up her sleeve. On her wrist she had a large bracelet of leather and a thin one made of gold chain. It had a tiny charm on it with a flat map of earth. If I could pick something that I would

96

want for myself, it would be that bracelet. How happy I would be with the Earth dangling on the edge of my wrist. A constant promise that even if I never returned, it was still home. I knew immediately I couldn't take it. It was worth too much.

"Quite a piece," I said. "I'll take the leather one."

But Els took the gold bracelet off as though to press it into my hand. It was the move of a person who was used to working people and getting what they wanted. I put my hands up in front of me so that the bracelet did not touch me.

"No," I said. "That's not how I work. I'll take the leather one."

Els's eyes hardened for a moment then softened again. She pulled off the leather cuff and handed it over to me.

I had a new piece of information now, too. This girl was tricky. She did not really want the lotion. We had been near each other for long enough for me to smell the soft scents that Els wore. She had luxury items already. She wanted something more.

I looked at the cuff and put it on my wrist. It was real leather. Worn and soft. Not fake. It was valuable as well.

Standing with Els made me miss Bitty. It was this longing that made me say yes to getting the lotion even though Els didn't need it.

"All right," I said. "I'll do you the favor."

"Goody," Els said. And then squeezed my arm the way my sister Bitty used to do when we were excited about something.

"But it might take a little while," I said. "It might be faster to get when you go to Bessen."

"Oh, that's not sorted out yet," Els said. "I need the lotion now."

"I'll need a bit of time," I said trying to calculate what favors and items I needed to do this in as few trades as possible.

"You could join us tonight," Els said. "Or I could join you."

I shook my head no, and she shrugged and turned and ran off to join the boys. I watched her. The way her black hair bounced as she ran. The way her curves filled out her clothes. The way she was so easy with herself despite being stranded on a space station. In all my time here, I had never been that at ease.

But I had the upper hand now in knowing that Els wanted something from me.

When Els rejoined the other Humans, they all looked up at me. I knew they were sizing me up. I tried to look unaffected by the attention. But it was the boy with the dark hair that caught my eye and made me catch my breath. He was looking back at me just as intensely—as though he already knew me—but neither of us smiled.

14

• •

The station had moods, and the next day I could tell
by the way people hurried by with heads down and whispered conspiratorial conversations that something big was
going on. There was a shift in the normal hum of the day. I
closed the metal curtain of my bin and tried to ignore the
excitement. But I could feel from the way everyone in the
underguts buzzed that whatever it was it was unusual. It probably meant some big cargo or some illegal entertainment
that was being run in the secret game hall. Or maybe it was
some kind of new drug that would sweep through the station
and make a few undergut dwellers temporarily rich. Or perhaps it was some information about the Imperium and their
new movements and conquests.

I placed the things that I could not trade in a day into a
secure box I had hidden in my bin and then went to the area
where we in the underguts dined.

Sometimes Heckleck would join me at mealtime, but
mostly he preferred to eat in private. The way he ate disturbed most species. I didn't mind his company because I
had become used to it.

When I first arrived in the underguts, I was never asked to
join the other aliens at mealtime. It bothered me at first to
eat alone. I had been so used to the constant company of my

family and the other colonists, but now it suited me just fine. I sat alone, eating meals while absorbing everything anyone said in the underguts. I had become an expert on the subtle body language of the different species. I could tell immediately when someone could be taken advantage of.

Keeping my distance was the way I'd survived. Now that so many aliens owed me favors, if I sat with one it might mislead the others into thinking that I had favorites. That would be a disadvantage to me, and I liked to minimize the odds against me in a deal.

It was an unspoken agreement with all the gutter dwellers to keep that table for me, so as always there was an empty table in the corner. Unless Heckleck joined me, I would eat there alone, head down, concentrating on the plate in front of me, eating every last morsel no matter what it was and be grateful for it. I was like everyone else in the gutter, never knowing when I might eat again so I always ate everything in front of me no matter if it was a protein pak or a real meal.

"A moment of your time?" an alien in the gutter dining hall asked. He'd approached my table uninvited.

I glanced at him. He had information he wanted to trade, I could tell. But was it information that I wanted? I didn't look up from my food. I kept putting the fork into my mouth, eating bite after bite. The alien hovered. I ate. He had thick legs, the size of tree trunks, and a tail that he balanced on. He started to shift his weight from side to side. That meant the information was good, and he thought it was valuable.

It probably wasn't.

When my plate was empty, I pushed it in front of me and then turned my eyes to him and stared him down.

He was a Minor Species. His snout was long. His nostrils opened and closed quickly. His clothes were filthy, and he had a sore on his forehead. I tried to figure out what he wanted. Coin? No. Medicine? No. Drugs? Yes. But he likely knew that I didn't deal in drugs. I reached into my pocket and took out a card. It was a chit for the bathhouse. There he could clean up and most likely make a drug connection.

"What's everyone so excited about?" I asked, motioning to the invisible buzz around the underguts.

"Imperium representatives found dead," he said.

"Dead?"

Dead was never good.

"Dead. Found stabbed and stuffed in a vent near where the Humans stay."

I knew that the other aliens were watching to see if his information was worth anything. A bathhouse chit was not worth much. He waited, hoping that I would put something else down on the table. After a few minutes, I put my hand out to take back the chit. The alien put his hand on top of mine. The deal was accepted.

"It's strange, don't you think, that the Imperium would not answer those Humans?" the alien asked.

"Everyone knows a message sometimes takes longer than expected to get a response," I said, "especially when there's been an emergency of some sort."

But that wasn't the truth. They should have gotten an answer by now from the Earth Imperium Alliance members on Bessen.

"Yes, of course," the alien said and bowed his head to indicate that I knew better than him.

Life was cheap out in the black. I had learned that, and it still hurt to know it. But those Imperium representatives being dead was trouble all around, and someone would be made to pay. I didn't want it to be me.

• •

Heckleck banged on the side of my bin with his appendage in the way that let me know that it was him. I pushed aside the curtain.

"Have you heard? A shuttle docked with two Imperium representatives aboard," Heckleck said.

"And now they're dead," I said.

Heckleck's mouth changed to a diamond shape, which after knowing him as long as I had, I knew meant that he was amused.

"Many would have killed for what they had. Look at this."

He pushed two data cards toward me.

"Travel passes," I said. "So what?"

"Not just any travel passes. These come with immunity. They cannot be questioned. They cannot be revoked."

"Impossible," I said.

I'd rarely seen travel passes. They were beautiful. They glowed with color and holograms. Then I realized that they were open passes. They gave free travel access to anyone to go anywhere any amount of times. Since travel was now so strictly regulated, these passes meant absolute freedom.

"How did you get these? Did you kill them?"

He probably hadn't. Heckleck was not squeamish about cutting off body parts, but he drew the line at murder. That was why I still did jobs for him on occasion.

"No," Heckleck said carefully. "I'm no murderer. Someone

who owed me too many favors was lucky enough to find the bodies first. Now our debt is settled and I have the passes."

"You'll get a good price for them," I said. "Plenty of takers for something like this." I liked the feel of them in my hand. I wondered what it would be like to be able to buy them myself. I could go anywhere. I could follow every lead until I found Brother Blue.

Heckleck leaned in and lowered his voice.

"I am not going to sell them," Heckleck said. "I'm going to use them."

I froze.

"Does that interest you?"

"Why would it interest me?" I said carefully.

"I could sell you one," Heckleck said.

I felt a rush of hope. With a pass like that I could go anywhere. It seemed like an impossible wish coming true. I had to be careful. Heckleck could be tricky. I tried not to show my excitement.

"I don't have enough currency on my chit for something as valuable as that," I said.

"I see that you have a bag of Brahar salts on your shelf there," Heckleck said.

"Yes, I do," I said.

"Well, what with the favor I owe you from yesterday, and the fact you gave me an extra trest, and that time that you went left in the corridor, instead of right, which gave me a distinct advantage with the representative from Per, I believe you've curried almost enough to earn you a pass. But I'll have to have that salt. I can see your mind already racing. You are not good at covering up your thoughts from me. You have always been set upon revenge."

"Not revenge," I said.

"Answers that if you get them will likely lead to you wanting revenge," he said.

"You'd get more from someone else," I said. I had kept a running tally in my head of favors exchanged between us, and while they were many, they were nowhere near the value of a pass that meant ultimate freedom.

"I knew you would say that, too." Heckleck said. "But I like you. And there is not much that means much in this world. But liking someone whose species you dislike is something—worth more than currency on a chit. Why don't you think about it? Or are you too afraid to leave the comfortable life you've set up here?"

My life here *was* comfortable. It wouldn't look like that to an outsider, but to me, it was familiar. I knew how to make it good. Out there everything was unknown. Places were unknown. Beings were unknown. I had staked my survival on knowing. Leaving, as much as I wanted desperately to do it, would be hard. But although the unknown was frightening, perhaps there was a different kind of life for me waiting somewhere out there in the galaxy. I reached over to the shelf and took the bag of salts down and gave it to him.

"All right," I said.

"There," Heckleck said. "This will be a great adventure."

"Where will you go?" I asked.

"Oh, I have my own questions that need answers too," he said. "But they can wait a little longer while I accompany you."

"You would go with me?" I asked.

"Well I can't very well have you leaving and traveling around without knowing how to get a ride on a ship, what destinations have the best light skip jump points, who is more amenable to taking on Humans, and how to get information that you require. No, no. Our tally begins anew."

"I will owe you," I said.

"You already do!" Heckleck said. "I have business to attend to in order to prepare. I want to leave as soon as possible, before more Imperium representatives come with their questions about the disappearance of the first ones. But I don't want to take the travel passes with me. They're too hot. Will you hold them for us?"

"How do you know you can trust me?" I asked. "I might sell your pass to the highest bidder."

Heckleck looked amused. As though he were proud that he'd taught me so well.

"It would only be for an hour or two," Heckleck said. "And then we'll be directly on our way."

"All right," I said. I took the cards and put them in my breast pocket.

"I always knew I could trust you, Tula," Heckleck said. "You're the only one down here I can."

It was a high compliment. Heckleck trusted no one. He closed the metal curtain behind him, and I heard him scurry away.

Two hours later, he still hadn't returned.

I didn't think much of it until the sirens started blaring.

"Raid!" someone yelled. "Raid!"

The law enforcers came, pulling down everyone's curtains and pulling people out of their bins. Before they got to me, I put my valuables and the passes into the tiny secret panel Heckleck had helped me devise when I moved in. I had just closed it when Tournour whipped open my curtain.

"Tula," he said.

"Tournour," I said.

"Will you come with me?"

His guards did not handle me roughly or pull me out. Tournour always made sure that his guards treated me with respect. I stood up and followed them. Outside, I joined all of the other petty criminals until we were all rounded up and brought up to the chief constable's office and detained. Tournour would talk to us all one by one.

I waited my turn and was relieved when I was finally called in.

"Your cutting has grown," I said.

"It thrives. Three flowers this year," Tournour said, "but no pollen."

"I've heard that it blooms all year on Quint," I said.

"Yes, I enjoy making a tea from the flowers," he said. "A rare delicacy."

I wondered if he'd ever been down there. I liked to think of Tournour smuggling a cutting back onto the station.

"I have news for you, and I don't know how one says these things to Humans in a kind way so I'll just say it. Heckleck's dead," Tournour said. "And I know that he meant something to you."

I wanted to cry out in pain. Heckleck just couldn't be gone. Not as quick as that. I knew that to get through the interrogation, I'd have to let myself forget my friend. Deep down, I knew he was dead because of those travel passes, and if I wasn't careful, I'd be dead soon, too. I would have to grieve for him later.

I composed myself.

"No one means anything to anyone down in the gutter," I said.

But it wasn't true. Heckleck had meant everything to me. He had been my parent, my mentor, my advisor, and my *friend*.

"I'm sorry to hear the news," I added.

"Do you know what he was into?" Tournour asked.

"Something bad, I guess."

"Did he talk to you today?"

"He talks to me most days," I said. "But I don't always listen."

"Did he talk to you about those Imperium representatives?"

"Everybody talked about those two." I was sure that was true, even though I'd only talked about it with him and the alien who had told me about it at mealtime.

"They had travel passes, and we need them back," Tournour said.

"We?"

"The Imperium," he said.

"If I had the travel passes," I said. "I'd already be on my way out of here."

"Of course," he said. "Tula, you didn't help him did you?"

"Help him what?"

"Kill those Imperium representatives?"

"No," I said. "I trade for favors only. Besides, as shady as some of Heckleck's dealings are, he never kills."

"Do you really believe that?" he asked.

"I know it," I said.

"They were Humans," Tournour said. "Did you know that?"

"I didn't see them," I said.

"I know you have issues with other Humans," he said.

"Do you think I killed them?"

"What do you know about a Human named Brother Blue?"

My blood froze.

"What does he have to do with anything?" My voice was rising.

"So you know him?"

"He left me here," I said.

Tournour keyed something into his datapad.

"Did he have something to do with this?" I asked.

"I'm just getting information to send my report to the Human Ambassador at Bessen."

How could Brother Blue be brought up at that same time as Heckleck was?

"Did he have something to do with Heckleck's death?"

"I'm not permitted to comment on current investigations," Tournour said.

"I'll trade you," I said.

He considered me.

"I think Heckleck cared about you more than I thought," Tournour said.

"Tournour, I'll trade you anything you want," I said.

"I thought the name sounded familiar," Tournour said. "This Brother Blue has a habit of leaving his Humans behind."

Without saying anything definite at all, I knew in my bones that he meant that Brother Blue had been here and he'd gotten away. I'd been this close to my revenge and hadn't known it, and somehow it had gotten Heckleck killed.

"Am I free to go?"

"You are free to go," Tournour said.

I made my way back to the underguts, and when I got

back to the safety of my bin I checked my hiding place. Nothing had been touched; my things, my currency chit, and the travel passes were safe.

Only then did I let it finally sink in that Heckleck was dead and if Tournour was to be believed, that somehow Brother Blue was involved. Heckleck had run things on the docking bays for years, and he was my only friend, the only one I trusted. Now he was gone. Heckleck had been everything to me. I hadn't felt this alone since the day I'd been left behind by the *Prairie Rose*, and now I had one more reason to hate Brother Blue. He must have wanted to leave badly enough to put himself in a position to be killed over those passes.

I locked the travel passes back into the hiding place. They were too hot to have any value now. The best thing to do would be to destroy them. But I couldn't. They were the only things I had left of Heckleck.

They were the only piece of hope he ever had. And they were the last gift he'd ever given me.

15

• •

For Heckleck, there would be no memorial.

I had no idea how a Hort was buried or eulogized. Here, on the Yertina Feray, memorials were mostly for those who lived in the above levels and had the luxury of grief. But in the underguts there was an unspoken superstition that to mark a death was to invite it to take you next. Heckleck likely didn't expect anyone to step forward for him after he died, although part of me wanted to mark his passing. But that was the Humanness rising up in me.

Out in space, on a ship or on a station, organic materials were rare and useful. I knew that when an alien died, if the body wasn't claimed, it was considered to be an organic compound that would be broken down and used where needed on the space station. To the arboretum to fertilize the greenery, or liquefied and pushed through the coolant system, or broken down into needed biocompounds in the med bay. Until it was determined that no one would come forward, send a message, or arrive on the station to do a memorial, a dead body was put into a cryocrate to preserve it until enough time had passed. If no one came forward, the body was recycled.

Cryocrates on the station were used for these kinds of preservations, but they were also commonly used by some species for interstellar travel. There was one hangar that housed all the dead bodies and sleeping travelers. Death and sleep have no distinction. Although I did not step forward for Heckleck, I spent that week sitting by his cryocrate in mourning.

I was not alone. There were a few others who sat with their loved ones, and there were medical personnel tending to the travelers who were being revived or being put into sleep stasis for a voyage. And so in the quiet, it was all types of Major and Minor alien species that sat in that hangar bay by the crates.

When they came to take Heckleck's body away for disposal, I steeled myself. I feared that it meant that I was doomed to die here, too. It hit me that when I did, no one would likely care to claim me or to sit with me before I was recycled.

With Heckleck gone, something changed. Perhaps it was the air of the station. As though the nanites no longer worked and it was harder for me to breathe. Or like gravity had been somehow made heavier. It was difficult to move sometimes. I covered less ground. I was much too overwhelmed with the burden of surviving my grief to admit that I was lonely.

I am supposed to be young, I thought. *I'm supposed to be carefree.*

Instead of those things, my thirst for revenge only grew greater.

Heckleck's absence was profound, but I never cried. I had given that up long ago. I found myself often going to the robot warehouse, to the miner robot that I had drawn a face on when Heckleck and I had explored the empty station together. The way that it sat there, with its tiny knife-like appendages and its back legs folded reminded me of the way Heckleck used to sit. I would confess my heart to the robot but no tears came, and instead of easing my sorrow it made it more profound.

He was dead. He'd been recycled. I gave myself a week, and then I buried my grief deep down inside of me. I did my job. I renewed my vow. I would work every favor until I got off of here so I would be ready to leave the day that the passes were usable again, slipping through when other Imperium representatives came to the station with other high-end travel passes. Until that day they were useless.

On my first day back doing my rounds, I noticed Tournour following me as I made my way down to the underguts. He seemed to materialize next to me on the walk back to my bin. Whenever he appeared like that, I wondered if he was making sure that I got home safely and that no one jumped me for whatever things I had hidden on my body. I said nothing to him, but I appreciated this smallest of comforts. I knew that company was a rare and elusive thing. It was one of the real treasures of life.

Tournour was quiet. We walked in silence, him giving me the time and space to think. After having to talk all day, I did not want to hear my own voice making small talk. Besides, I didn't have much to say to Tournour anyway. We were worlds apart. Usually I would walk away alone, always aware that he watched me until I disappeared from view. He never ventured into the underguts unless he was conducting a raid.

When we reached the last level before the underguts, he stopped at the threshold and spoke.

"I'm sorry that he's gone," Tournour said. "He was something to me in my life and I will miss him."

Then he walked away.

• •

At the arboretum later that day, I did as I always did and I took off my shoes and sank my toes in the dirt, leaning my head on the window. Quint kept its power to soothe me. We were coming up on its equator. I liked to look at the line that cut across the largest of its continents, like it was wearing a thick belt. Thado had explained to me that it was the growing belt. Most of the planet was made of shale and other rock, but that belt consisted of the only place on the planet where anything could grow. It was one of the reasons why Quint had always been a poor candidate for settling, and why once it was depleted, it did not thrive.

"That's the Dren Line," a voice said behind me. "Very fertile at one time. Now useless."

I turned. It was the young man with the blond hair.

He stepped up next to me.

"Don't harm the plants," I said, thinking that he might not know to not trample the precious plants.

My tongue felt strange not speaking Universal Galactic. I sounded foreign, as though I had acquired an accent.

"Never," he said.

We watched in silence as the vast ocean came into view.

"I'm Caleb," he said. He stuck his hand out. "Caleb Kamil." I ignored it. He put his hand down and leaned his head on the glass. "And you are Tula."

I nodded.

113

"I heard about your friend," he said. "I'm sorry for your loss."

I hadn't thought of that. That they might be asking as much about me as I had about them. In the last week I'd all but disappeared with my grieving. Here was a person who, having recently lost so many himself, likely understood my pain. I appreciated that he did not press or talk for a while longer. He just stood there with me, staring alongside me at Quint. I realized that what I missed most about Heckleck was his presence, so I was quietly grateful for this Human's. Somehow, perhaps because we were of the same species, he was able to intuitively understand how I needed to be comforted, with silence. I was thankful, but I would never say that. It struck me that perhaps I didn't have to.

Finally, he spoke again.

"It's here that I had the first chance to look at another planet. Of course, we saw the planets in our own solar system on our Earth Imperium Alliance Youth Academy space training exercises, but going by light skip doesn't really allow for sightseeing."

"It's strange, isn't it?" I said.

"To be so far away . . ."

". . . And yet really only to have seen the blackness of space."

"Yes," Caleb said. "Exactly."

"Quint isn't a planet that anyone on Earth would know about," I said.

"But it's the first planet I've seen, and I want to know everything about it," Caleb said. "I've been learning about it. It's almost like that planet is my . . ."

"Friend?"

"Exactly."

I allowed myself a smile. Probably the first one since Heckleck died.

"There is a plant that blooms on the planet," I said.

"The alin? Yellow flowers. Very rare."

"I have one."

"You do?"

"Yes."

"I would love to see that."

I stopped myself from offering to show it to him. A part of me wanted to show appreciation to him for this moment. Perhaps it was just a normal Human thing to do.

I stopped looking at Quint and turned to look at him. I had not seen many true blonds in my life. Everything about him was pale, except for the dusting of brown spots on his face. *Freckles.* I remembered how my sister Bitty would get them on her olive skin when in the sun. When I looked at his eyes, they were not alien. They were eyes I could understand how to read. Now gentle. Now thoughtful. Now amused.

"I saw you talking with Els in the market," Caleb said.

"Yes," I said. "She needed an item."

"What kind of item?"

"A personal one."

He smiled and suddenly I couldn't tell if it was genuine or if he was trying to get something out of me as well. That sobered me and immediately my guard went up.

"I don't discuss my deals," I said. I became all business.

"Of course," he said. "I apologize."

He put his hands up in front of him in an apologetic gesture. I knew it to mean that he meant no harm.

We'd been standing there for over an hour. I had nowhere to be, but it made me realize that I should get back to my life. There were things to be done, and if they weren't done, I would lose all that I had built when Heckleck was alive.

Tomorrow I would begin the hustle again. So I leaned my head on the window.

Caleb began to hum. It was that song.

"I know that song," I said. I hummed a bar along with him. "I haven't heard any Earth music since I've been here. Not until your lot came."

And then he turned to face me and began to sing.

> *Fly the ocean in a silver plane*
> *See the jungle when it's wet with rain*
> *Just remember till you're home again*
> *You belong to me.*

There was nothing much more to say. And then the moment was over as he shifted away from me, breaking a thread that I suddenly noticed had stretched between us.

He nodded at me in a parting gesture and walked away.

16

· ·

That night I dreamed of Earth.

The sun was in the sky. My dress was snagged on the spines of a cactus. I was caught and could not undo myself. And someone, in the distance, was calling my name.

Tula!

In the morning when I awoke groggy, I felt strange. Dreams brought up long-forgotten memories and situations that felt real; as though I were living parts of my past again.

After such a particularly vivid dream, I did not feel hungry but knew from the times that I had gone hungry to always eat when I could, regardless of the desire. Near to Kitsch Rutsok's, I headed in and ordered a protein pak.

"Can I join you?" a voice said. It was Reza, the other Human male. The one I'd yet to meet formally.

He sat down without waiting for a response. For some reason, instead of annoying me, I admired his boldness.

"I'm Reza," he said. "Rumor has it you're the person to go to with impossible requests. And I don't mean luxurious lotions."

I said nothing. I didn't have to. In time he would ask for what he wanted himself and name the price or favor that he wanted to trade. But he didn't say a word. I changed my tactic and broke my own rule of engagement and spoke first.

"Do you need something?"

"Not yet. But how about I'll come to you when I know what it is?" he said.

I nodded. He was dark. Everything about him was dark. His hair. His eyes. His skin. When I looked at him, my pulse quickened.

"We're stuck here just like you now. We might as well try to get along," Reza said.

"Is that what you think?" I asked. It came out playful sounding, instead of wry.

"Yes," Reza said. His smile widened. He had a nice smile.

I lifted up my hand to order another protein pak for him. When it arrived Reza slurped it down quickly and loudly. He was starving. That told me that they must be low on currency. When he was done, he crumpled up the foil pak and he leaned back on his chair as if to take me all in.

"We have a difference of opinion about whether we have to get along," I said.

Reza smiled again, and we sat in silence for a while. It was a different kind of silence than with Caleb. This one had sparks to it. I felt like smiling, but I kept the curious feeling of happiness in check.

"You're not very likable, are you?" he finally said. It sounded like an insult, but his eyes were twinkling. He was teasing me! And I was enjoying it.

"Everyone here likes me," I said, indicating with a sweep of my arms the aliens surrounding us.

"Everyone here, but I doubt you'd find any Human to say that they liked you."

"Why would I care about that?" I asked.

He laughed. I liked his laugh. His mouth opened very

wide. He clapped his hands loudly together. His eyes squeezed shut. He touched his stomach and let his breath out.

"I haven't had the occasion to talk to a Human in a long time," I said. Part of me wanted to touch his arm when I said it, but I didn't because I'd learned to touch an alien could ruin a deal. And though he was Human, he felt alien to me.

"Do me a favor and talk to Els," he said leaning forward, as though he were trying to close the distance between us. "She can't stop grumbling about the fact that you're ignoring us. She's better when she's fed."

"You too," I said. "I noticed."

"No," he said, laughing. "I mean when her desires are being met. Right now it's whatever you're not getting her. She said she's paid."

"She did," I said. I lifted my wrist to show him the leather cuff I was wearing.

"Then just give her what she wants," he said. "For my sake."

I nodded. It was as though we were a team.

"I've been preoccupied," I said. "My . . . friend died."

"I heard," Reza said. "I'm sorry."

"Thank you," I said. I should have gotten up to leave, but somehow I wanted to stay. The playfulness of sitting with him was now gone and replaced by a more serious air between us, but it made me feel closer to him. I looked at him, and though I felt sad, I smiled.

"Good, I knew that we'd get along," he said smiling sweetly back at me.

"I still don't know that," I said.

"But you like me, right?" he said. "What does your gut tell you?"

I sized him up. His eyes were warm. He was smiling. His

arms were crossed, but not defensive. *Guarded*. But I did kind of like him.

"You don't look like someone who cares if I like you," I said. "Besides, what does it matter?"

"It's much more pleasant when people like each other," Reza said.

"I wouldn't know."

It was his turn to size me up. I allowed him to get a good look at me. I was used to being sized up.

"You're not very Human," he said. "And I hear you're a little bit in love with that planet."

"I'm not likable. I'm not Human. What am I, then?" I asked.

Strange. I'd known him for barely any time at all but it seemed as if I'd known him my whole life. Everything about him, the way his eyes half shut when he smiled. The way he chewed on his lower lip. The length of his fingernails. All of it was familiar to me.

He was so different from Caleb and from Els. Caleb was soft, fragile. Els was so put together. But Reza was open and wore all of his emotions on his sleeve, and he was solid and strong. It seemed as though nothing could push him down, as though nothing could rattle him.

"I don't know. *Alien*. You have the walk of a Loor, the laugh of a Hort, and the smile of a Per," he finally said.

"The smile of a Per?" I asked. Maybe he was insulting me. But he wasn't. He was being playful again. I relaxed.

"Well, they don't smile do they?" he said. "And you are the least Human of all the Humans I've ever met."

"Humans aren't very nice anyway," I said. "Nobody likes them . . ."

"Us," he interjected. "Us. Me, you, the others, out here. That's us."

I did not want to belong to that "us." But I nodded.

"Us," I said. I could not deny that I was Human.

"All that is changing, now. We'll be more than just a species that roams or an isolationist planet. We'll be more settled and less unknown. People don't like the unknown. The Earth Imperium Alliance is set to integrate with the Children of Earth colonies and welcome Humans who roam. Humanity could expand. Things should be better for us out here."

"Integration?" I asked.

"You're one of the colonists, I heard," he said. "What was your colony?"

"My destination was Beta Granade," I said.

"The fifth colony," Reza said. "Yes, one of my friends was to lead the integration at that colony. But he didn't make it."

"Well, I didn't get there," I said. "And no one is at Beta Granade. The colony ship meant to go there, my colony ship, the *Prairie Rose*, exploded."

"I can assure you that there is a colony there," Reza said. "Otherwise Brother Blue would not have listed it as one of our colonies."

"No. You are mistaken," I said.

"We were on our way there, to help with changing over of the infrastructure of those colonies to get them up to Imperium standards."

"That's impossible," I said. "Brother Blue never wanted his colonies mixing with the aliens or wanderers other than for remote trades."

"Brother Blue is the architect of the plan," Reza said. "He's the one who negotiated the treaty with the Imperium and formed the Earth Imperium Alliance."

Brother Blue was no longer just a cult leader on the fringe. He had all of Earth at his disposal. Things snapped into place. He'd known. He'd known that the Imperium was coming, and then he'd sold out the *Prairie Rose* for his benefit.

"Brother Blue? From the Children of Earth?"

"Yes," Reza said. "He knew about the imminent take over and convinced Earth to vote in the Earth Imperium Alliance and to take advantage of his colonies as a bartering chip. It was either that or the Imperium would mine Earth for resources. But with the colonies united with Earth, we were able to negotiate a deal as a promising species."

"Brother Blue," I asked again, to make sure.

"I heard him give a speech once," Reza said. "He's a most persuasive speaker."

"Yes," I said. "We all believed whatever he said."

It came out sounding even more bitter to my ears than I thought I was.

"He is a man of his word," Reza said, trying to defend him. "He's the reason why the Imperium made its offer to Earth. There is no more Children of Earth. Brother Blue dismantled it and helped to create the Earth Imperium Alliance. As I said, we were set to integrate with the few Human colonies that the Children of Earth had managed to settle to make them Imperium. But our ship was destroyed, and now that goal of integration is in peril. Word is that Earth Gov has regained power over Earth again. There will likely be a civil war. And though the Earth Imperium Alliance is trying to work for Earth's best interests from Bessen, now we can't seem to reach even them. Earth Gov already considers anyone with the Earth Imperium Alliance traitors, but now even the Earth Imperium Alliance thinks we're traitors as well. They think that someone on our ship sabotaged the ship in Earth Gov's cause."

I excused myself. Nothing Reza could say now could bring back that playfulness we'd shared earlier. I was too filled with hate.

17

- -

I sat in my bin and stewed. It ate at me, Brother Blue being out there among the stars, free to do harm with no consequences. And now these Humans came saying that Brother Blue did a great thing for Earth. I saw the way that Reza talked about Brother Blue.

It was with *admiration*.

My rage was at a constant boil.

Brother Blue had sent them here. These Humans were with him. Any softening of my feelings that I had toward these Humans had changed. But I knew that in order to expose Brother Blue for the fraud that he was I would have to ingratiate myself to the Humans. They were in his pocket, and so I'd have to be in theirs. I went about the business of getting Els the item that she wanted.

There were many steps to procuring a specific item. It was easier when I had things and could let people know what was available. It put me in a weaker position to have to get one specific thing. Which is why, for what Els wanted, I found myself bartering with a Monian.

I slammed my fist on the table and stood up. I leaned in close to the Monian, and I opened my mouth as big as I could so he could stare inside my throat. It was an act of submission, and it was respectful. Of course, my throat had none of the things that a Monian throat had, but the alien before me went through the motions, coming in close, putting his eye right up to my mouth. I tried not to gag as his oily forehead brushed my lips.

The Monian stretched his neck out as high as it would go to show me that he knew what was really on the line: *Reputation.*

My business with him was done. Five more transactions and I found myself in possession of a substance that would substitute for what Els likely thought of as lotion. She'd have to accept it; everyone had to make do out here with substitutions.

I got word to her to meet me at the Temple of the Gej. The Gej's temple was the most architecturally beautiful thing on the station. It was full of arches and statues and shrines to gods and places that no one knew.

I had once asked Thado about the Gej. He told me that the Gej had not been seen for over a hundred years. They were from the farthest edge of the Outer Rim and were a highly spiritual people who kept to themselves. When they had been on the Yertina Feray, they had thrived. Once Quint had dried up, they had retreated back to their quiet part of space, but their temple still stood.

I loved to retreat to the temple. It was often empty, and it was my second favorite place on the station. Sometimes, when I'd procure an object I did not know how to trade, I'd bring it to one of the shrines and place it as an offering. I liked making offerings to gods I did not know. It seemed somehow more pure. Did the Gej have one god or many? Were they even gods at all? I wasn't certain. But when I put a cracked gem down or burned a sole stick of incense, it calmed me as if I was wishing on fallen and forgotten stars. Perhaps

I'd given a gift to a deity who cared only for love. Perhaps I'd placed a trinket on a devil. I couldn't be sure, and I didn't care.

Els was late. I heard her arrive by her loud footsteps echoed in the vast hall. I didn't turn around.

"This place is wondrous," Els said, stepping in front of me.

"Yes, it's good for singing," I said.

"Singing?" Els said. "You don't look like a person who sings."

"Every species sings, even if it's badly," I said.

"You would know better than I," she said. "But that will change once I've been out in space long enough."

I could tell by the way that she stopped to mess with her hair that it bothered her that I could say something about aliens with authority. I could tell by the way that she kept adjusting her shirt that she was concerned about how she looked, not just to me, but to anyone. It was her main concern. Her hair was perfectly brushed, not a hair out of place. Her clothes were crisp and complemented her form perfectly. She was wearing makeup, not the light amount like my mother used to wear, but a whole lot, as though she were wearing a mask. She was tilting her head in a way that seemed submissive, but could have been posed. I wondered suddenly, if she had been late on purpose. I had used that trick sometimes, to make my contact agitated.

I took my time getting the lotion out, stretching out the moment to take my advantage back. It worked. Els looked impatient as she waited for me to speak.

"I have something that might suit you for your skin," I finally said.

I passed over the small pot and watched as Els opened it and inhaled the smell. She smiled and then dipped her finger into the substance and rubbed it on her hands.

"This will do just fine," Els said.

It was different talking to Els than it had been talking with Caleb or Reza. Whereas Caleb had a warm energy and Reza was electric and gave the straightforward impression that what you saw was what you got, Els was cold. This confused me, and it made me uncomfortable. I could read a plethora of alien species, but it'd been so long since I'd been with Humans that I was having trouble figuring out what these differences about them meant. If I listened to my gut, it told me to be on my guard with her. I quickly looked to see if it was possible that she had a weapon. She didn't. But there was something about her that made me put all of my walls up. I knew that she didn't really need the lotion.

I was torn between leaving or staying to learn more about the divided situation on Earth with the Imperium and Brother Blue. But I knew from experience that when you wanted to run was the time to stay. I focused on what my long-term goal was: to see if I could leave with them when they left. *If* they left. And get them to take me close to Brother Blue so I could kill him.

I let no part of my body language betray that I wanted to leave. I dug in and stayed only in this moment.

"Have you tried it?" Els asked.

"No."

Els dipped her fingers into the pot.

"Your face is dry, right on your forehead," Els said.

Els reached her fingers out as though to touch my face. Involuntarily, I backed away.

"I'm not going to hurt you," Els said.

With the exception of Caleb grabbing my elbow to help me up, no Human had touched me since the *Prairie Rose* left me. I forced myself to relax, and then let Els put the lotion on my face. The touch shocked me. I felt alive. The lotion felt cool and nice. Els worked the lotion into my skin. Her fingers were gentle.

"Sit," she said.

I did as I was told and sat on one of the pews. Els put her bag on the ground and opened it.

"Don't you ever brush your hair? Or wash it?"

"Who would care?"

"*You* should care."

"Aliens don't really know what a Human is or isn't supposed to look like," I said.

"But you do," Els said.

Els began to brush my hair. The bristles on my head felt nice. She pulled on the tangles that my wavy hair always knotted into. I closed my eyes. I remembered my mother brushing my hair when I was little. There was the pull on the knots, my head arched back, and then after a bit of tugging, the strokes smoothed.

"It's so nice to hang out with a girl," Els said softly.

I wanted to feel the same. But instead I put my hand up to my head to make Els stop.

"Am I hurting you?" Els asked. "I thought I got all the knots out."

"No," I said. But in fact, Els was hurting me. Hurting me with memories that drifted up, memories of my mother and sister who were now long dead; making me feel as though I was supposed to look a certain way when that kind of thinking or feeling didn't have anything to do with me anymore.

Els came around and sat on the pew next to me. She draped her arm over the back of the bench.

Now I wanted to leave. To run, really. I wanted Els's arm off of my shoulder. But actually sitting and talking with a girl again was intoxicating to me. I could not pull away. I just wanted to watch her and be in her presence. Even though I did not know her, her exaggerated Humanness, the way she wore her clothes, the red of her lips and cheeks, the browns that accentuated her cold eyes, felt strangely compelling to me.

She seemed to be in such sure control of herself and of me.

"Earth Gov thinks we betrayed them. And the Earth Imperium Alliance thinks that one of us is a traitor," Els said. Then she looked up at the dome and then back down. When she did, Els's eyes were suddenly full of tears. They were perfect and flowing, but they didn't seem real. Still, somehow seeing tears tugged at me. My heart cracked because sadness looked so familiar even though I myself had not been able to cry in so long. I tried to remember what to do. The last person I saw cry was Bitty. I had pulled Bitty in for a hug and let her sob on my shoulder. I did not want to hug Els, but I knew that a touch would be appropriate. I lifted my hand but found I could not touch Els. I let my hand fall back into my lap. But Els had seen the intention of my gesture and grabbed my hand to her.

"If only one of us could get to Bessen and explain the situation to Brother Blue directly, I'm sure we could clear this whole mess up," Els said. "I've spent my whole life trying to get to the stars. I won't get stuck here. We're not traitors. We're not with Earth Gov. We're supporting the Imperium. If we had a travel pass, then I could go clear things up."

And there it was. I froze. I kept my face as neutral as I could. What did she know of the passes? Who had been talking? Only the alien who owed Heckleck the favor knew that he'd had them. It would be normal for that alien to think that I knew something about them since Heckleck and I worked so closely together.

The passes would be useless until another Imperium aide came to the Yertina Feray. Only then, hidden among newly distributed ones could the old ones be used. But the Yertina Feray was on the fringe of the Imperium so that would likely not happen for a long time.

"Passes for free travel are impossible to get," I said.

Els cocked her head to the side.

"We were supposed to meet with representatives from the Imperium to discuss our predicament," she said. "But they never showed up for the meeting. I think you know why."

Because they were dead. The Humans hadn't killed the representatives. Why kill someone who was going to give you something you wanted? I wondered if it had been Heckleck. But why?

"And Brother Blue? Were you to meet with him, too?"

"If he had been here then this could've been straightened out right away," Els said. "He's the head ambassador to the Imperium."

Brother Blue had not been here after all. Tournour had just reported the deaths to him. It only slightly soothed me that I had not missed my chance to kill him.

"Some things are just impossible and best forgotten. Like those passes" I said.

"Surely someone owes you that kind of a favor?" she said. She was using flattery in a way that I had never found effective with aliens.

"No one ever owes anyone *that* kind of a favor," I said.

"You should appeal to the Imperium again. They take care of their own."

"But someone must have those passes," Els said. "And I could use one."

"Just you?"

"We," she said, correcting herself.

"Everyone here has somewhere else they want to be," I said.

"I think that those passes were meant for us," Els said.

For a moment, I thought of Heckleck and my heart twisted. He was still so freshly gone.

Els took my hand again. I cringed. Not because I didn't like the hand, but because of the intimacy that it inspired. But hopefully Els didn't notice I was uncomfortable as she closed her fingers around mine and leaned in closer. After a moment, I relaxed into the game. It was a game I'd played a million times before to win a deal or a favor. Her grip was strong and steady, and it reminded me so much of my sister that I felt the urge to tighten my own fingers around hers.

"Earth is silent now as it struggles with its interior problems. The Earth Imperium Alliance at Bessen is debating our status."

"Have you tried reaching the colonies themselves?" I asked.

"I have messages to the Children of Earth colonies pending as they were supposed to receive us. But they are silent," Els said.

"Did you ever speak to them?" I asked. "When you were headed to them?"

"All of our communications to the colonies went through Brother Blue," she said. "I worked in communications and everything was a go for our arrival."

"But did you speak to them yourself?" I asked. I needed to know.

"On our last light skip, as we were to approach the colony on Andra we were told to divert to wait out a massive solar storm."

"So you never made it to a single colony?" I asked.

"No. Our ship exploded."

I found it interesting that every message to the colonies went through Brother Blue. That was consistent with what we experienced on the *Prairie Rose*.

"There was so much smoke, and parts of the ship were being sealed off," Els said. "We were lucky, we three made it to the escape shuttle. But everyone else died. Reza grabbed me so I wouldn't follow our crewmates out of a hull breach. I owe him my life."

"You're lucky that Reza saved you," I said. "That's a big favor to owe. Humans sometimes push, instead of pull."

Or punch. Or kick. Or spit, like Brother Blue.

The evening chimes sounded. Els's hand flew to her mouth.

"Oh! I'm late! Reza has us all on Sunspa rotation. He's managed it somehow."

As she ran off I wondered if, when the *Prairie Rose* disintegrated, anyone had tried to make it to the escape pod. They'd all done drills in case of an evacuation, but I supposed in the moment drills would be forgotten. Perhaps someone was still alive, on a station like the Yertina Feray or on a planet somewhere. Alone, like these Humans, dependent on the kindness of a bitter gutter dweller like me. Or what if Reza hadn't been mistaken? What if some of them had made it to Beta Granade somehow? My heart skipped a beat.

18

· ·

With all of this new information I was at a loss to figure out a course of action, and it made me miss Heckleck. He was always full of knowledge on what to do when no one path seemed clear. We'd spent many an evening swapping tales about our days.

What made me freeze each time I tried to think of a course of action was the fact that Brother Blue had risen so high. It was impossible to think straight.

I went to the warehouse, to my confessor, the mining robot with the painted-on face. I sat in front of it, willing it to be Heckleck. I tried to summon him up in my thoughts and to figure out what he would say to me about the Human situation.

He would tell me to look at the facts. I had the passes. They were valuable despite not being useful right now. He might remind me that they could be more valuable if I gave them to others for a bigger favor or sold them for a smaller return. He would ask me to try to see the bigger picture. One week down the line. One month. One year. Five years. Ten years. Twenty. I made myself dizzy with the thoughts of that many moves ahead. I was not a master as Heckleck had been.

"I hate them," I said, even though it was not true. I did not hate Els, Caleb, and Reza. I hated that they confused me. I hated that they had dealings with Brother Blue. That they had been close enough to stab him and they didn't.

Why would they? They didn't see him for the true terror that he was. They saw him as a man who had Earth's best interests at heart and as someone who could help them. It was infuriating. I lashed out and kicked the robot in frustration.

The robot did not change expression. It had no sage advice for me. It did not care that I had lost my temper. I touched its cold metal to forgive it its failings and to thank it for forgiving mine.

I reminded myself that if I watched how things played out, if I left them to their own devices, something useful might present itself. That was what Heckleck had always said to do. Always play long, never play short.

Eventually, something would break.

I watched and took it in over the next few days. Els hung around Kitsch Rutsok's bar trying to ingratiate herself to any alien that she thought had a connection to the Imperium. Reza spent hours at the Ministry of Colonies and Travel, pumping tokens into communication devices, making calls that my source there informed me were still only met with silence. Caleb hung about the docking bays for reasons I couldn't figure out. They were bad at trading. They were bad for my business. Their situation was getting worse.

Which was why it was no surprise when a few days after meeting with Els an alien came into the dining area and yelled, "There is a commotion in the luxury ring!"

Commotions often happened, and they were always announced because the lowest of the lowlifes saw it as an opportunity to steal or take advantage. I ignored the exodus of aliens leaving their plates and protein paks half-eaten on the tables. Some would go and steal. Some would go to watch. When there was a lack of hochts, commotions were a kind of entertainment, especially if they involved one of the rich falling to join us in the underguts.

"Who is it?" one of the lazier aliens called out. I knew him to be interested only in certain kinds of commotions. He could not be bothered with basic domestic disputes.

"It's the Humans," the alien called out.

I took my time. I finished eating. I drank some recycled water. I cleared my plate. Then I walked slowly to the lift.

The lift doors opened, and I could hear the crowd. The aliens were mostly standing around and jeering. The Humans were being escorted out of the home they'd squatted in. Tournour was leading them out. Reza was arguing heatedly with Tournour while Caleb was trying to calm him down. Els was crying and shaking and trembling at the roar of the crowd.

The aliens were screaming and howling with delight. The alien next to me was cursing and it didn't matter that they were Humans, what mattered was that pent up frustrations were being released. I remembered helping him when there was a complication with the birth of his children. I couldn't help myself, I punched the alien's arm. He turned to me mid-holler ready to strike, but when he saw who it was, he stopped. I gave him a look and a gesture that to his species meant to stop and I'd be in his debt. He got the message and began to shush those around him. Then he helped to make a pathway for me to get a closer look at the action.

I pushed to the front. I could see Tournour, who always

kept his calm as he did his job. He looked like someone who was taking out the trash. Tournour saw me in the crowd and made his way over to me.

"I don't suppose they're being escorted to an Imperium ship," I said.

"You know they're not," Tournour said. "They've over-stayed their hospitality up on this ring and run through their currency. They are terrible negotiators, and no one will claim them."

"Can't you disperse this spectacle?" I said.

"I didn't think you cared," Tournour said.

"I don't," I lied. "But when you kick others who've fallen to the underguts, you do it quietly."

Tournour turned back to look at the Humans.

"When there hasn't been a hocht in a while, it's good for the population to let off steam," Tournour said.

He walked away from me. I cursed him with the only Loor slur I knew under my breath, hoping that he would hear. I watched as he spoke to one of his guards. The officers immediately shouted out some orders, and soon officers started pushing back the crowd and clearing them from the ring with threats of arrests and round ups. This opening up of space around them calmed the Humans.

Before I left with the crowd so that I wouldn't get arrested, Tournour caught my eye and nodded at me as though he'd done me a favor. I knew what it meant. I owed him.

I cursed. Likely, this favor owed wasn't worth it.

19

. . . .

I next saw them wandering the gutter, poking into bins trying to figure out how to secure a spot in the underguts.

I sat in my bin, metal curtain open, watching as Els, Caleb, and Reza stumbled and fought for a place. They were very bad at it. They picked the wrong people to approach. They were misled, taken advantage of, and given the runaround. Reza tried the hardest, and if it wasn't for him they would not have managed the mid-sized bin that had hardly enough room for all three of them. I knew that it would not be comfortable. As the lights dimmed for Final Chimes, I closed my metal curtain. I listened to the familiar rhythms and the sounds of the underguts as everyone settled down for sleep. Only this night, Els's loud sobs added to the cacophony before the quiet. It grated on me, and I suspected it was meant to pull on my sympathies.

The underguts was not at all like the upper decks. It was dank and dark and it smelled. I remembered how frightened I was my first night down here.

A few hours of sobbing passed, and then there was silence. I wonder if Els had gotten bored with getting no response or if the boys had managed to calm her or if it was something else. *Adaptability.* Even I had grown accustomed to my lot in life once it had changed. That was a gift. It was what made the Human species strong. It was what had made me strong.

. . . .

I was used to others staring at me as the station's sole Human. I'd always been strange to the people that lived here, but this morning as I walked toward the Nurlok's fabric shop the stares were more evident. And worse, they were coupled with whispers. I passed by and aliens stopped. I caught sight of an arm or a tentacle or an antenna turned in my direction. Mentally, I scrolled through all the transactions that I'd done in the past few days and tried to figure out if I'd handled something badly. Had the rules changed? Had I offended someone? Had the chain of trade caused something to sour? It was important for me to figure it out in order to nip whatever this strangeness toward me was in the bud. My status had to be impeccable. All I had was my word and my reputation.

The Nurlok was standing in front of his store, sucking on a long smokeless pipe. One of his children was hiding behind his legs. The child kept peeking out at me and then screaming in that way that all children do when they are both afraid to look at something and daring themselves to look at it. The child was excited at its own bravery. I knew that it was because as a Human, I looked like one of their culture's demons.

"Tell me again which one of your sex is the stronger or the weaker?" the Nurlok asked.

"That's not a fair question," I said, wondering what kind of test this was.

"I know you to be strong, but what of the others?" the Nurlok asked, smoothing over the perceived offense.

"I think we are all weak and we are all strong," I said. I did not want to admit that there was a time in Human history where women were called the weaker sex.

"My money is on you," the Nurlok said.

"Thank you," I said and I brought a box out of my pack. The Nurlok slid open the wooden box and examined the Jurniarn slug I had procured.

"It's small," the Nurlok said.

"Yes, travel was hard on it, I think," I said. "But it's pregnant."

The Nurlok emitted an agreeable noise.

"Let's see its quality," the Nurlok said, taking his pipe and poking at the slug. The slug turned from brown to yellow and started to puff out. Soon a thread came out of its mouth. I looked away and noticed there was a hocht poster up on the wall behind him, but I couldn't see it closely. They were everywhere.

The slug continued to spit out its thread. The Nurlok took his pipe and scooped it up and began to feel it with his fingers. He held it up to the light. He showed his child and explained things about the slug in their language. The Nurlok was pleased with the strength and the color of the thread, but said that the feel of it was not the most desirable.

"The quality of it might be changed with care and diet," I said.

"We have an agreement," the Nurlok said. "You have three bolts of whatever you might need as a return favor."

I'd wanted four, but three was a good price. I nodded.

Then he put his pipe back in his mouth and lit up the coil. The sweet smell of whatever it was he smoked came out. I took my chit for the future bolts and glanced at the store window where another hocht poster hung.

After I read it, I understood why everyone had been staring at me and why the Nurlock had asked such strange questions about Humans.

HOCHT

The Human **CALEB KAMIL** calls a hocht on the Human **TULA BANE**

★ For not behaving in a Human ★
manner in the deep of space

★ For not lending aide to ★
Humans in distress

Betrayal of Species ★ For her silence

"Have the bets begun?" I asked.

"Yes," the Nurlok said. "The odds are not in your favor."

"I would think my acquaintances would know that I could hold my own."

"No one knows anything about Humans," the Nurlok said. "The rule of thumb is to bet on the being who calls the hocht. They are the more passionate. They want to win more."

"Of course," I nodded.

I had not played this right.

20

....

If they wanted to win a hocht, why Caleb? Reza would have beaten me easily; he was large, physically fit, and obviously very strong. Even Els had more observable physical strength than Caleb. Caleb was skinny, and he seemed fragile as though even a look could break him. Perhaps it was to trick me into thinking that I could win? If that was the problem, I couldn't begin to guess at their motivations.

Why?

Why would he do that?

Yes, I had stayed out of their way since they'd moved to the underguts. But I had not done anything to truly offend them.

But deep in my heart I knew I had. I had ignored them. I had not inquired after them. I had not helped them in any way. I had not behaved like a Human being.

On the day of the hocht, I could hear the people as the lift doors opened to the main level. I didn't remember ever seeing a hocht so well attended. The square was buzzing. I weaved my way through the gathering crowd. It seemed more busy than usual. People cleared a way for me. Some aliens nodded at me, some looked me over as though they were trying to determine whether they'd made the right bet.

I was nervous, so I'd come late and missed the earlier

parts of the festival. I approached one side of the hocht ring. Caleb and the other Humans were on the other side. Reza was leaning in close, presumably giving Caleb advice on how to beat me. I wished I wasn't alone in my corner. I wished I had someone to hold a towel for me. Heckleck would have done that for me. I wished he was here to tell me what to do—to tell me how to see the win in this. I was afraid of fists coming at me. I looked around in the stands for a friendly face and was surprised when I saw that Tournour was sitting in the back row. He was with a female Loor, and they were sharing a twisted germy.

He was with her, but unlike her, whose eyes and antennae were focused on him, his were focused on me. When he saw me looking back at him, hoping for a sign of encouragement, he moved in closer to the female.

Then something pulled at my hand. It was the Nurlok's child. She was there holding a bottle of water and a piece of fruit. She had a towel in her hand.

"Thado sent this over," she said. Her voice was tiny and nervous. I took the fruit that she held out to me. It was full of sweetness. I had not been able to stomach any food this morning, and so it felt good to have something to fill me. I knew I would need sustenance to get through the hocht. My eyes searched until I found Thado, and I held up the pit of the fruit in thanks. He nodded back to me. It was a comfort to know that Thado and Tournour were here for me, even if they were not in the ring with me.

I took the bottle of water and drank a gulp down. It was good water, not recycled swill, but premium kind, imported. It was a little more sulfur tasting than I liked, but still, it was a treat and I was grateful. The little Nurlok flipped open a stool and encouraged me to sit. Then she went buzzing about, shooing people away as best she could to give me enough room to think.

I thought about the fight. I had learned a few things about fighting during my time on the station. There had been a few scrapes. I'd learned how to hiss like a Nurlok. I'd learned the spot that makes a Loor pass out. I'd learned how to crouch and bite like a Hort. But I did not know how to use my fists. They frightened me. They were capable of harm that I did not want to inflict on anyone else.

Caleb got into the ring. He was stretching. His bones looked even more fragile than I had remembered. He skin was covered with freckles.

I did not want to fight him. I considered throwing in the towel. I could forfeit and then we could meet without the crowd. They could barter with me as though they were a client. I could only imagine that this was about the travel passes. It was a measure of desperation. Perhaps they thought they'd be able to scare them out of me.

"Go, go," the little Nurlok said.

I got into the ring. I crouched on the floor. I breathed in deeply. I listened to the crowd. They were getting louder. Some were chanting my name. I stood up. I stared at my opponent. I stood perfectly still while he stretched. Caleb began to slyly catch my eye. He would lean his arm over his leg and then he would glance at me. Every stretch, he glanced and held my eyes a little longer. Where first I saw a determination in him, now I saw hesitation.

Neither of us wanted to be here.

That gave me hope.

I remembered the fights I'd gotten into as a child. They

were few. There was hair pulling with my friend over a doll we both wanted. There was a slap and a push I gave to my sister, Bitty, when we were fighting. There was a kick to the groin I'd given a boy at school who had tried to paw me at a party. Then I turned my thoughts to the fights I'd witnessed. My father, drunk over the holidays, fists in front of him, always jabbing at my equally drunk uncle, face covered with his arms but his stomach getting pummeled. I remembered the bully from school, Mika, fighting the scrawny Stan: Mika moving quick from side to side while Stan crouched low, always hitting Mika's spleen. And of course Brother Blue, standing over me and kicking in my ribs.

I assumed a position, crouched low with fists in front of my face. I didn't know if it was a position of power or weakness, but I was determined that I would not go down. Caleb had gone to a military academy, and despite his skinniness, he had likely learned to fight. He had been trained.

Don't think. Just do, I thought. *Just keep standing.*

The bell rang. The hocht began. We moved toward each other and began to circle. I kept up my stare. He swung. I dodged. He swung again, I dodged. I saw an open spot on his face, and I punched. My knuckles connected with his chin. It was a soft punch. It did no harm. He sprung back, more surprised than hurt. I crouched again, and he swung over my head. I hissed at him.

He pushed me.

His hands landed just above my breasts. He pushed me again. I put my arms up to him. Both of our hands were on each other's chests. He pulled me in, crooking my neck in his elbow.

I had never been this close to a man. He was sweating.

Our skin stuck together. It made a noise when we pulled apart and came back together. His mouth was near my ear, his breath hot. He had some stubble on his cheek. His skin was warm. His smell filled me. He pulled me in tighter, and I tried to slide out of his grip. I wanted to both pull away and also pull in closer but my eyes kept going over to Reza, who was watching from the side. I stumbled backward, wishing that I was doing this dance with him (although if I were, he would have already beaten me). Caleb came at me and I stamped on his foot and brought my knee up to his groin. He yelped and let go. The crowd cheered. We went to our corners. The Nurlok girl gave me some more water. I watched as Caleb toweled down. Reza and Els were whispering in his ear and watching me. Reza kept shaking his head from side to side.

Reza glanced at me in my corner and gave me a weak smile. He was with me even though he was over there. That was a comfort.

In a hocht there are no rules, no time outs, no referee. Every fight was up to the two combatants. And between Caleb and I there seemed to be an agreement. This was a fight, not a beating and that made a difference to me. I did not cower. We came together and fell apart four times, each of us landing punches that hurt the other; each falling toward the other, almost waltzing and then pushing each other away with a flurry of painful blows.

The fifth time we came together I knew one thing; I could not keep it up for much longer. I was weakening. And though I could see that he was tired, Caleb was not. I started toward him. I put up my hands. They were bloody and they hurt. My eye was swollen. My lip was cracked. My breath was labored.

He pushed me. I stumbled back. He pushed me again. I swung and stumbled toward him. His arms were around me, holding me up.

And then he yelled in my ear.

"Come on," he said. "Is that the best you've got?"

That jarred me awake and to action. I snapped my eyes open as he pushed me off of him. We circled each other again. He nodded at me. And then he looked down at his own body. My eyes were blurred by sweat that fell in my eyes. He yelled again. And then I noticed. He was doing most of the moves, but he was showing me where there was an empty space to punch him.

My hand struck. He doubled over. He showed me his jaw. I hit him. He circled me exposing his spleen. I jabbed. I kicked him. He fell to the floor, doubled over in pain. I kicked him. I kicked him. I kicked him again.

"Enough!" yelled Reza. He threw a towel into the ring. The crowd erupted in cheers and began to shout my name. The hocht was over. I had won.

The little Nurlok came over to me wrapping me in a large piece of fabric. I was shaking. Every part of my body hurt. But I also felt alive in a way that I had not felt in many years. I looked over my shoulder at Caleb. It was a powerful feeling to defend one's honor, and I had done it. He was leaning on Reza. They both looked at me sympathetically. It was Els who was the most unhappy, yelling at the both of them as they moved away.

The little Nurlok nudged me toward the crowd. People were pressing in on me. Some were shouting, angry that I'd won. I had been the underdog. But some were joyous, because they had won money. The Nurlok tried to clear a path but was too small to be effective. And then Tournour was there. He was in front of the crowd, parting it for me. He was alone; the Loor female he had been with was nowhere to be seen. He put his hand under my elbow and helped to keep me steady.

"Go to the med bay," Tournour said. "You need stitching up. He got you good."

"I should have lost," I confided to Tournour. "He let me win."

"I know," Tournour said. "But I made a lot of money betting on you, so I'm glad he did."

Suddenly I was at the lift and Tournour blocked the way so that I could go up alone. I leaned my head against the cool metal of the elevator and made my way to the med bay.

The doctor brought me over to a bed and gave me a shot. "Tsk, tsk," she said. "You Humans leak so much when your skin is broken."

I would have to rest for several days.

All the parts on my body that hurt began to numb. But not my heart. That was still beating strong.

21

• •

The announcement came at Sixteenth Chime. The station would be passing through a meteor shower, the remnants of a comet that no one had seen for centuries. The angle at which it approached meant that we would be taking a fair brunt of it.

Along with everyone else, I headed immediately to my designated shelter. When I got there I checked in, so that my whereabouts were accounted for, but once accounted for, instead of pushing through the door with the crowd, I moved away.

There was a reason to go to a shelter. It meant life in case of disaster. If one of the meteors punched through the hull, the station could get decompressed and if you were caught outside of the shelter, you could die.

But there was no better time to get loose annoly wire than during a lockdown. The probing sensors opened to monitor even the most microscopic fissures, foreign elements, and radiation levels. The wires from the previous opening fall away, exposing the new wires. The dropped wires were still good and worth something for their scarcity. Annoly wires were a good thing to barter with, they were needed for many tiny repairs, but not easily obtainable in small quantities. Technically the loose wires belonged to the station, but the ones that fell were considered fair game to my mind. They were usually just swept up by the cleaning bots as garbage during the lockdowns, which is why no one ever managed to get any. By the time everyone emerged from the shelters, the wires were long gone.

It wasn't stealing. I didn't steal. If I collected them, I would have something that was hard to get and more valuable than them being swept up to be melted. If I was going to commit to getting off the station sooner than later, I would have to take risks.

The danger, of course, was that being caught outside of the shelter was against the law and if the meteorite or radiation got through, potentially dangerous. Heckleck had always said that it was lucrative but not worth the possible high price. A fool's harvest, perhaps. But things had changed, and I needed to have every advantage.

It was spookier to be wandering around the quiet of the station now than it was when when the Imperium had first come. Perhaps it was because then, there were still aliens moving about their days. But now, the halls were empty in a way that signaled the immediate danger. I could see some of Tournour's unit checking doors and quarters, making sure that everyone had evacuated. They were wearing full space gear as a precaution against the elements that might rip through the surface at any moment. Seeing them covered head to toe was unnerving. I shrank into a nook to avoid their sweep. When they passed, and the lights of the station powered down, I knew that I was alone, and they had likely gone into a shelter themselves. It was too late to beat on a door of a shelter to let me in—I'd made my choice, I had to hope that I'd live through it.

The chimes stopped, but a pulsing emergency light kept a steady beat. I moved to the first sensor probe, and there, as I had expected, were some wires on the floor. I swept them up, careful not to prick my skin, and put them in my bag.

I followed this course, staying just ahead of the cleaning bots. My haul was pretty good, and I tried not to get too confident about what the wires could do for me.

After the fifth probe that I hit, I began to forget about the pulsing light and began to enjoy the silence. I felt like the last woman in the universe. It was then that I heard it. A noise.

I froze. I could hear the shower. It started small and then increased in intensity. The meteorites slapped then evaporated against the hull like a heavy hail storm. My fear was palpable. I wondered if I would hear if one pierced the exterior, or if I would just expire. But nothing changed, and soon I became used to the gentle steady hail of meteorites. I even enjoyed the rhythm of them.

My guard was completely down, so that when I turned a corner, I was unprepared for what I saw.

At first I thought it was a ghost. I could not process that I wasn't alone. But then, when my brain was able to make sense of what I was seeing, I saw that it was Caleb. He was near a sensor, but he was not interested in the wires. He was helping himself to some electronics from a storefront that had been left open and unattended when the owner had evacuated. I froze in place, stupidly thinking that he would finish what he was doing and then go in the other direction, not noticing me. But when he turned to move he smashed right into me.

He let out a yell. My bag fell to the ground, wires fell everywhere, mixing with some of the parts he'd had in his hands.

"What are you doing here?" he yelled. "You scared me half to death."

His voice sounded unnaturally loud against the now lessening noise of the meteorites against the hull.

"I could ask you the same thing," I whispered.

"It's dangerous to not be in a shelter," he said as he kneeled down next to me. I felt strange being close to him again after having just fought him in the hocht.

"You're not invulnerable to the dangers of space either," I said.

On our hands and knees we tried to separate out our things.

"Why call the hocht?" I finally asked.

For all of the bruises still left on my body, my feelings were what hurt me most.

"It was Els who called it," Caleb said.

"Els?"

"Yes," he said. He looked uncomfortable. "Els thought that a hocht would be the best way to see what you were made of, to see if we could shake you into helping us."

"And you and Reza agreed?"

"She didn't consult us," he said. "She signed me up and then told us. Reza and I were against it."

"If she had the grievance with me, she should have fought me," I said. "That's the way a hocht works."

But I knew why. Els didn't pay attention to the way things worked. She paid attention to the way that she could get things to work for her. She didn't sign up Reza, because Reza would surely win against me. It was cunning and smart of her to force Caleb and me into the ring. It would look like an even fight.

"You could have said no," I said.

"Sometimes it's just easier to do what Els wants," Caleb said. "I think that's why Reza and I are alive. We followed her when the ship was disintegrating."

"She said you both saved her," I said.

"Els has a habit of misremembering things. I think it's because she grew up dirt poor and had to hustle her way into the Earth Imperium Alliance."

I could not argue with that. Survival made us owe in strange ways.

"How did I measure up?"

"You didn't. Look, Reza and I should have come to you right after. We don't want you to think that we have anything against you. And I'm sorry if I hurt you."

"I'll live," I said. But I was touched by the apology. It seemed sincere.

"The three of us, well, we're at odds on how to get ourselves off of here or what we should do. We're supposed to be the youth branch of the Earth Imperium Alliance. That's why I left Earth. I thought that was Earth's best chance. But things have changed. This voyage. The explosion. Things that don't add up."

"What things?"

He turned to me, as though perhaps if he spoke it out loud I could make sense of it for him.

"Earth was torn between joining the Imperium or staying undeclared."

"But they joined the Imperium," I said.

"It was that or be unprotected," he said. "Mined, taken over, depleted of resources, and abandoned. What would you choose?"

Earth had so long been in a struggle to rebuild itself after the droughts and the pandemics. To have it all swept away by the Imperium would be devastating.

"I don't know," I said.

"The Imperium means life," he said. "We are protected. We have trade. Things look bright. Brother Blue was right there to sweep in and save us."

I made a face at Brother Blue's name.

"But not everyone feels like that," I said.

"No," he said. "There are people on Earth who believe that the best thing would be to resist the Imperium and now they are back in control. And I couldn't understand that before. I made my choice, but what if it was the wrong side?"

I had no response to that. He took a handful of wires from the ground.

"Those are mine," I said.

"I could use these," he said. "I'll owe you one."

"Fighting me was not the way to win a favor," I said.

But still, I tried to calculate the worth of the wires against the promise of him owing me one. He didn't know their real value, and I could tell that he just needed wire, any kind of wire. But before I could say no, the strobing lights stopped. I tilted my head, straining to listen. There was nothing. We were through the shower. The all clear signal started.

I had to get myself in position to mingle with those emerging from the shelters. I didn't have time to say yes or no. I went my way, Caleb went his. He'd made off with some of his stolen goods and half of my wire.

I wondered what he needed these things for.

I didn't quite make it into a nook before I was caught by one of Tournour's people.

Tournour looked at me as I sat in the brig. He had my bag of wires and a few of the gears that Caleb had taken that had accidentally made themselves into my bag spread out on a table in front of him. He looked disappointed. His antennae kept folding up and down as he looked me and the items over.

"Stealing?" Tournour said. "It's not your style."

"Those aren't mine," I said.

"I know they're not," Tournour said. "They belong to a very irritated shopkeeper."

I was in the brig. Caleb was not. He likely hadn't gotten caught. I had two choices: I could rat him out, or I could protect him. I wanted to rat him out. I wanted the wires and the worth that they represented. But Caleb would never be able to get Tournour to let him go. He'd be tried and he'd be guilty and he'd be in the brig for months. I could strike a deal and be gone in no time at all.

"They had fallen when I was taking the wires near the shop, I must have accidentally scooped them up," I said. I wasn't lying. That was exactly what had happened.

His antennae moved in a way that let me know that he knew I was not telling the whole truth, but that he was willing to buy it.

"So you're remorseful," he said.

"An accident," I said.

"The shopkeeper is willing to let this accidental taking of his property go in exchange for all of the annoly wires you've collected," Tournour said.

I started. That was too much. My entire forage would be

155

for naught. I wanted to yell at the unfairness of it, but as I stepped up to the bars, their hum of electricity reminded me where I was and that if I didn't play this right I could be there for a long time.

Begrudgingly, I nodded.

He swept all of the wires and electronics into the bag.

"Good," he said. "Then there is the matter of your breaking evacuation protocols."

I sighed. Perhaps I'd never get out of here.

"Three days in here and then you can go," he said. "After all, according to station records, you were in Shelter 5. And my records show that there was only one Human who was not accounted for and failed to check into an evacuation center."

He knew! Tournour knew that Caleb had been out there, too. But that was the way these things worked. As long as a Human had been reprimanded, everything was even.

22

. . . .

After my three days were up, I went and found
Caleb. He was sitting in his bin hard at work on a tiny piece
of electronics. He was leaned over, lost in focus as he
smelted something. Reza was reading a datapad. Els was
nowhere to be seen.

I banged on the side of the bin. Caleb's fingers slipped,
and I could tell from his curse that he'd ruined whatever he
was doing. Good.

"You owe me big," I said.

He didn't agree or disagree with me. He put his work
down. He looked at Reza who shrugged and then went back
to reading. It stung me to be brushed off by him, but I was
here for an explanation from Caleb.

"Come with me," Caleb said. "I want to show you something."

I followed him, wondering where he could possibly be
taking me. It was when we started to get closer to the more
derelict parts of the station that I began to have a hunch. And
when he jimmied the door open to the warehouse full of the
mining robots, my hunch was confirmed.

"How do you know about this place?" I asked.

"I get restless," he said. "I walk a lot."

He brought me right up to my robot, the one with my face markings.

"This is the only one that turns on," he said. "See the face? Someone knew that."

He reached behind the robot and flipped a switch. The robot came to life. It was rudimentary, but it was moving.

"What did you do?" I asked. It came out like an accusation, but really I was impressed.

"I'm restoring it," he said, "to be a companion of sorts."

"You already have companions," I said.

"I might not always have them," he said. "I might not want to go where they want to go."

"You're going your own way?" I asked. That's what he was doing at the docking bays. He had a plan to escape from here. "Where do you want to go then?"

He moved in close.

"Can I trust you?" he asked.

I stayed quiet or else I would tell him that I could not be trusted.

"If I were to speak to you with my heart, then I would say I want to go to Bessen. But it's not there I want to go. And the reason that I would go to Bessen is not for the reasons that you think. I do not want to ingratiate myself to Brother Blue."

"What are the reasons to go to Bessen if not that?" I asked.

"Love."

"Love?" That was unexpected.

"A girl. Myfanwy. We spent the summer together, and then we were assigned to different ships. She was sent to help with the growing Earth presence and to help at the Embassy on Bessen. I was sent to coordinate with Earth from a colony. And well, now I'm here."

"And you haven't seen her since Earth?"

"No."

"And you still love her?"

"Yes."

He took a tool and adjusted a gear on the robot. The head moved up and down.

"Have you communicated with her?"

"No," he said. "Communication is nearly impossible from this station."

"Does she know that you're here?"

"Yes, I assume she does."

"And she hasn't helped you?"

"Myfanwy is the reason that I look at the sky. She is the reason why I love the stars. She is the reason for my ambitions. I won't rest easy until I see her again. And I know that she loves me. I know it in my heart."

"You didn't answer my question."

He looked at me sheepishly—as though he were a bit ashamed of himself. I wondered what it would be like to love someone that much. To me it seemed to love someone that was absent would be like loving the notes of a song. They could envelop you and make you feel, but those notes would never be real. Then again, what did I know of love? I couldn't remember the last time I had loved anything or anyone. And I had certainly never had feelings for someone in a romantic way. But then suddenly I thought of Reza and wished I were somewhere alone with him.

"So where do you want to go then?"

"The Outer Rim," he said.

Once again, he'd surprised me with his answer. I'd thought perhaps he wanted to go back to Earth, or to the Human colony he'd been assigned to.

"You're running?" I asked.

He evaded the question.

"Why do you want to go to the Outer Rim?" I asked. "Why remove yourself from the center of the action?"

"This has always been about how to save Earth," he said. "Earth needs help to extract herself from the Imperium."

"Then join with Earth Gov. Show them that you are on their side," I said.

"They won't have me, and I'm not sure that they are the right alternative," Caleb said. "Besides, Earth Gov is old-fashioned in its way of thinking about being a world in the galaxy."

"Agreed," I said. "It's bigger than that. The Imperium needs to be taken down."

Those words could get us killed, but they were true. The Imperium was strangling the galaxy. Perhaps being so far out had protected the Yertina Feray from feeling the full effect of the Imperium, but it was still choking us. There were fewer ships who docked here, which meant fewer trades and fewer goods. The administrators left behind may not have been a military presence, but the amount of datawork to get anything done had all but paralyzed the functionality of the Yertina Feray. And then, while no one said it, there was a distinct lack of certain Minor Species. And every ship that did dock brought rumors of colonies and planets of those missing Minor Species that suddenly went dark.

"If I find Minor Species willing to strike down the Imperium from the Outer Rim, then perhaps . . ." Then he stopped.

His shoulders slumped. He became quiet. "But I'm not a leader," he said.

"Aren't you?" I asked. "A youth officer in the Earth Imperium Alliance? Isn't that why you were selected to help a colony make the change over to integrating with Earth?"

"No," he said. "I had no interest in becoming an officer. It just happened. I'm smart enough, but not the best. I'm lazy. I like to be comfortable. Els is a leader. Reza is a leader. But I'm not. I prefer to follow orders."

He seemed so sad and small, just a poor boy in love with a girl at the other end of a galaxy. Too frightened to actually go to her side. Too frightened to take the fight to Earth where it would demand too much of him. I felt sorry for him.

"I've watched you, and *you* are a leader," he said. "I observe the way you weave through this station. You command respect."

"So I did measure up at the hocht," I said.

We both laughed.

"No, because you do nothing with your potential. You waste it. You don't choose a side. You believe in nothing," Caleb said.

"I believe in myself."

We were silent for a while.

"I need parts," he said. "That's why I was out during the storm. Right now the robot can only walk and use its mining tools. I know I owe you, but I'd owe you even more if you'd help me get the parts I need to finish fixing it up and help me get out of here."

I looked at him trying to see down to the very bottom of him. I could not find a lie. He looked as though he were telling me the truth.

"If I go my own way to the Outer Rim, I'm not going to want to be alone."

I put my hand out to touch the robot. The metal, though cold, somehow seemed warm and alive. Perhaps because, in its small way, it seemed alive to me since it was the only thing that knew all of my heart.

I liked seeing it move. I had always wanted it to be fixed.

"Don't ever get rid of its face," I said.

"I won't," he said.

"I'll get you parts," I said. "But I can't help you leave. If I could do that, I'd go myself."

"Thank you."

I tried not to think about how much I would miss that robot if Caleb ever actually managed to leave this place. The odds of that happening were so remote that it seemed fair to bet that the robot would never go.

23

There were rumors that the station had not gotten off so easily from the meteor shower and that significant damage had occurred to the communications relay. Tournour and his officers kept the peace, but due to increased dissatisfaction their presence was more marked since the meteor shower. They even had their tiny two-shot phase guns clearly on display as a show of power.

The Yertina Feray always seemed to have poor reception, but now it was down to near silence. As isolated as we were, messages needed to come out and in. Worse, ships could not hail us to dock. The normal low quality had always made everyone grumble, but it was as though the whole station were blind now. You could feel the panic about it as everyone tried to maintain a sense of normalcy while living in a crippled place.

Maintenance needed to be done. Now. If the crew didn't get outside and fix things, everything on the station would fall into disrepair. Disrepair was never allowed on a space station. It meant death.

But somehow, the station was slow to react. Aliens clamored outside of the Ministry of Colonies and Travel, desperate to communicate with their planets. Even I, though I had no one to send messages to, was feeling a sense of panic without my routine listening to chatter. There had been comfort in paying to hear the public radio communications from Earth and the pre-broadcasted messages from the Children of Earth colonies, even if those messages meant no salvation for me.

I was bartering with the shopkeeper who had taken all of my wires for a certain ball bearing piece that Caleb needed when I noticed Reza hovering near me. It bothered me. I could not help but feel his eyes on me. It made me aware of the movements of my body, as I gesticulated with the shopkeeper. Did I look ridiculous with my hands waving in the air wildly? I did not want Reza to think I looked ridiculous. The shop-keeper's species negotiated not only with their voice, but also with their gestures. Self-conscious, my gestures were off and so, instead of four perfect grade-A silver balls, I got three tarnished silver plated balls. Caleb had Reza to blame for it.

I walked toward Reza, deciding to take a direct approach.

"Don't you have something better to do than watch me?" I asked him.

"The way your hands move, it's beautiful," he said. "Al-most like a dance, like a flamenco."

"I don't know what that means," I said. But it thrilled me that he thought something about me was beautiful because standing this close to him, I felt charged. I'd been wanting to see him. He'd been in my thoughts.

"It's a compliment," he said.

He then began to gesture in such an awkward way that if I were the shopkeeper's species I would be violently insulted. I grabbed his hands to make him stop. His hands curled over mine.

"What do you want?" I asked. His fingers played with my skin.

"This communications problem," he said. "I have to hear what's going on back home. If I'm going to go back there to try to help Earth Gov see that joining together makes humanity stronger, then I need to know everything. I need to hear the chatter. There is likely a civil war brewing on Earth now that the Earth Imperium Alliance is trying to regain control, and I'm flying blind here. It's driving me crazy."

"You're not the only one," I said, pointing to the gathered crowd outside the Ministry of Colonies and Travel.

"But all they can do is yell. I can help," he said. "I can fix this."

"The dishes are outside," I said. "You can't just hack your way to making it better no matter how good your Earth Imperium Alliance youth cadet training was back on Earth."

"No, I mean, I'm trained for EVAs and communications," he said. "That's my specialty."

"So?"

"Get me a spacesuit," he said.

"What?" I said. "You want to go out there?"

"I told you I'd ask you for what I needed when I needed it. This is what I need. Get me a spacesuit, and I can probably fix the array. Get me two, and I'll get it done for sure."

"You want two spacesuits?"

"Yes, one for Els and one for me," he said.

I wondered how many trades I'd have to do to get two working spacesuits. I stared over Reza's shoulder as I calculated. It would be challenge. I liked the idea of a challenge. It made me feel alive in some way. And if I could do it, Reza would be impressed. As strange as it was, I wanted Reza to be impressed with me.

I nodded.

Besides, the station was dragging its feet. They were waiting for experts to come and assess the damage; there were bids from different species to get the job. It was taking too long. If I helped Reza to fix the array, then everyone would owe me just a little more. Helping him helped me.

"What will you give me for it?"

"Besides communication?" he asked. "When I succeed, I'll have clout on Earth."

I almost said that wasn't worth anything, but then I stopped myself. Heckleck had often told me that things that seem worthless have a way of being the exact thing that one needs in a pinch down the line.

I nodded and then walked away. I knew exactly where to start. Thado.

It took me twelve trades to get the spacesuits. They weren't the most modern model, but they would work, and better yet, with only a few alterations, they would do for a Human.

• •

It was not easy to get off the space station without authorization. Reza and Els chose to exit from one of the docking bays when a small ship was leaving. I went and joined them with the Nurlok who had agreed to tailor the suits. I watched as Reza and Els suited up with the help of Caleb. When they were dressed, they tested their air supply and did their final checks. Reza turned to me and gave me a thumbs up.

Caleb, the Nurlock, and I stepped into the safe zone as the air lock shut. So many things could go wrong. It made me wonder why Reza and Els would purposely put themselves in harm's way on the remote chance that they could fix something. It seemed irresponsible. But I had contributed to the folly.

The outer door opened, and Reza and Els stepped out into space.

"Come," the Nurlock said.

We walked the station, finding the windows that would allow us to see their progress. Reza was wearing the suit with the red stripe and Els, the one with the blue stripe. The Nurlock, Caleb, and I had earbuds in and could hear their communications. They were all business.

Slowly, as we watched, others gathered. Aliens everywhere began to notice that someone was outside the station. Throngs crowded together, pressing themselves against the windows.

"Looks like you've got an audience," I said to Reza.

He turned away from the main dish, slowly rotating until he faced the station window. And then he waved.

"It's a pretty view of Quint from here," he said. "I bet you'd like it."

I loved how self-assured Reza was. He looked comfortable floating in space while he worked, and it made me happy to watch him doing something that he clearly did well. He was in his element, and that made him seem like he was the only person worth paying attention to. I felt proud that I knew him and that I had helped make this happen.

"Stay on task," Caleb said into his communicator.

"Finalizing and reinitiating dish start up," Els said.

"Three . . . two . . . one . . . engage," Reza said, getting back to work.

"Moving to dish two," Els said.

They went to every dish checking them out. By now the entire station was clued in to the fact that Reza and Els were out there. Caleb was standing near a window, biting his thumb. He looked more worried than I was. Despite wanting something totally different from each other, in a crunch or crisis, they had all three come together. I felt a certain pride in that. Their repair job did more for Human alien relations than anything.

"It's working!" The aliens came out of the ministry. "The dishes are starting to communicate beautifully. It's never been so clear."

There was a united cheer from the station. And the panic that had been so steady in the air lifted in relief and celebration.

"What's going on here?" Tournour appeared next to me. I turned to him and grabbed his arm excitedly, pointing at Reza, floating by our window.

"Did you help with this, Tula?" he asked.

I nodded.

"You are all violating around thirty different rules and station protocols."

Reza and Els had moved onto another array and had given the signal that it was working as well. The crowd around us cheered.

Tournour took in all the joyfulness around him.

"Didn't you say to me once that the Yertina Feray takes care of its own?" I asked.

He shook his head.

"This wasn't smart," he said. "I should throw them in the brig. Dangerous. Stupid."

"But you won't."

"Are you protecting them? Are you protecting him?" He pointed outside the window at Reza.

"They're doing what you couldn't get done," I said.

"Is that what you think?"

"It's what I know."

"You're so naïve sometimes, Tula."

Embarrassed at the fact that two Humans had taken matters into their own hands, Tournour made the call to the maintenance crews who then suited up themselves to take over the EVA operation from these upstart Humans. Reza and Els would not be punished. They were relieved of their mission and sent back inside.

"I have to go find Reza," I said.

"Why?" Tournour asked.

"To thank him."

Tournour's eyes narrowed and his antennae stopped moving.

They had gotten the job done where the Imperium could not.

It felt like a first victory.

24

. . . .

I remembered what my mother had said when I was
growing up. If a person had been rude, they should try to
make repair with an offering of some kind. The truth was I
felt bad about how I'd handled the Human situation. I
wanted to start over with them. They had done a great thing
for the station.

I could not go without a present. I unstrapped the items
that I'd procured during the day, but rejected them. None of
them were quite right. I opened my secret panel, pushing
aside the passes, knowing they would be the best gift, but
not something I would ever consider giving away. Besides,
the passes still held a glimmer of hope for me, and I didn't
know whom I would choose to take the spare one. One
thing Heckleck had often told me was to hint at the possibility of yes to everything and everyone and then to sort it
out later. I wasn't sure in whose hands the passes would be
best utilized, but I think I could cross Caleb off the list.
When I did go, if I managed it, we were headed in different
directions.

Wherever Brother Blue was, it definitely wasn't on the
Outer Rim.

I slid out a beaded light. It was pretty and practical. It

would be appreciated and seen as a gesture of warmth and goodwill.

I pushed the curtain aside and made my way to the alley where the Humans were staying. It seemed quiet.

I announced myself.

"It's Tula," I said, rapping on the side of the plastic to make my presence known.

The curtain pulled aside. I expected to see them all huddled in there together. But it was only one of them. Reza.

"Hello," he said. "Come in. What a nice surprise." He put the datapad he was reading aside and patted the place next to him.

He was not lying. He was glad to see me. He extended his hand out to me in a friendly gesture. I took it and we shook. His hand was warm. I didn't want him to let mine go.

I hesitated but realized that I was the one who had come. I stepped inside and sat down.

"Where are the others?" I asked.

"They've moved."

"Moved? How did you manage that?"

"Funny thing if you help fix a space station. People give you things," he said and then handed me a bottle of premium water. I took it when I noticed that he had a case of it.

"Haven't you moved, too?" I asked. The water was sweet and cool.

"No," he said. "I've made a split from the others."

"Why?" I asked.

"We're going in different directions. That was getting us nowhere. I want to go home. To Earth. On my own, I think I'll get there."

Suddenly I saw him, gone from here, on his way to some-where else. He had a certain determination about him that I didn't see in most people who were stranded here. I didn't even always see it in myself.

"Yes. You look like you have the luck about you."

"Thank you," he said. "I think we need to regroup and go home to Earth. Back to the beginning."

"That's what my father used to say," I said.

I was still holding the beaded lights in my hands.

"What's that?" he asked.

"It's a gift."

"You've come with a gift?"

"I thought perhaps for Els."

"Ah," he said. "She's taken quarters up in the upper decks."

"Of course," I said. Els liked luxury in everything. Lately I noticed that Els had started wearing alien fashions of high quality. I often saw her up at Kitch Rutsok's on the entertainment level, laughing and going to parties.

"What about Caleb?"

"He's four aisles down by the coolant vent."

"Bad spot," I said.

"Caleb doesn't negotiate well," he said.

That made me laugh. Which made him smile.

"She'll like that. She does have a taste for the extravagant," he said taking the lamp.

"Why are you and Caleb still down here and not up there?" I asked.

"I'm not settling in. I aim to leave. A place like this . . ." he indicated the bin, "is temporary."

That was what I had always thought. And yet I was still

here, living in miserable conditions, saving my comfort for later, when I'd be gone. But I had been here so long I began to wonder if that day would ever come.

"It's nice to be in this bin, alone," Reza said. "Don't you ever want to be alone?"

"I've been alone a long time," I said.

"I'm sorry," he nodded. "I'm sorry that you've been here all alone for so long. I've never been alone."

"You must not mind it," I said. "I imagine you joined up."

"I had no choice," Reza said.

"Someone forced you?"

"My father. He always told me that a man 'had to have a future! Have a cause!' His cause was to take advantage of the Imperium's generous offer to Earth and to become rich. Gain power. I am a pawn in his cause. Offer the son to the galaxy to prove you are true."

"So you're an isolationist," I said.

"I don't know what I am. I just know that Earth is my cause, and the best way to help her is to be there, on the ground. Not here, in space."

"I have no cause, and I'm better off for it," I said.

"You're a colonist," Reza said. "The Children of Earth had a cause."

"It wasn't my cause. It was my mother's," I said.

We had both lost people to the blackness of space. His open face played a symphony of feelings and finally rested on a look of grief.

"Is that why you stayed behind? Because you didn't believe in what the Children of Earth were doing?"

"I didn't stay behind," I said. "I was left."

Reza's face was open and eager to hear more. He moved

his body, making room for me, and I found myself moving in closer.

"Tell me," he whispered.

It was a part of my mind that I kept a tight lid on. Everything that I remembered about that time I had long ago pushed so far down and sealed up inside of me. Even just remembering the alarm on the ship as we light skipped to this system made me queasy. I remembered the colonists gathering on the main deck of the ship, asking questions, and Brother Blue assuring us that all was well, just a minor hiccup in the annals of space travel.

"We were with Brother Blue," I said. "We were onboard, heading to the colony when a message was received. Or there was trouble. It wasn't clear. We were diverted to the Yertina Feray."

Reza put his arm around me. His eyes were dark and sympathetic as he listened.

I went on to explain that once we'd docked with the Yertina Feray, we were instructed to not wander the station. Brother Blue did not want us to see others. We were told to keep to ourselves in the docking bay.

"I'd never seen an alien before I stepped onto the Yertina Feray," I said.

"That's normal. They are rarely on Earth and when they are, they rarely venture out of the big Earth cities," Reza said.

"I suppose the fear of being so far from home kept everyone in check. Everything was strange. And stepping off the ship and onto the deck of the Yertina Feray made everyone skittish. We'd really left home. We really could not go back."

"It seems strange," Reza said. "As the youth cadets of the

Imperium, we are encouraged to learn and meet with others. Brother Blue wrote the handbook. I wonder what Brother Blue was trying to protect back then."

"He told us that we were building a new Earth where we were going. No need to be influenced by the other kinds of thoughts. He told us that aliens despised Humans, and that they would kill us for who we were. Stay together. Stay safe."

Reza stared at me as though he understood, in a flash, everything about why I had been so suspicious of them since they'd gotten here. I closed my eyes. I felt sick. Thinking of Brother Blue and telling my story made me feel awful.

"But I had taught myself a little Universal Galactic, and so I was taken to meet with Brother Blue about a job. It was the worst thing that ever happened to me. He left me here to die. He beat me, and he left me here."

Reza's hands cupped my cheeks. I opened my eyes, and his eyes were so close to mine that I could see the biology of the iris. We were so close to each other, and I could hear his heart beating. It was a different beat than when I had been close to Caleb's in the hocht ring. Reza's heart was in time with mine.

His lips were just inches away from mine. I was on fire. As Reza spoke, I could feel his breath on my face, and I opened my lips hoping to catch his words in my mouth.

"When I saw my father return home from Bessen, he was a changed man," Reza said. "It was as though greed had wormed its way right into the very core of him. What was I to do? Say no? I was his son, and he ruled my world. He had the power to make my life easy or miserable. I was told to join the Earth Imperium Alliance and no longer associate with my isolationist Earth friends, and so I did. And now,

I've been left here too. My own father won't even help me. He's chosen power over family. He thinks I'm a traitor."

Every part of me reached for him. I ran my hands through his hair. He smelled kind. I had no words for pain, for despair, for loneliness. I put my lips on his.

Our hands found each others' skin. My body trembled. I had to stop before I exploded.

"I should go," I said. I was too overwhelmed by the physicality of Reza. "I have rounds to do." My mood had changed. I shifted my body away from him.

I had gone hungry at times during my time here, but truly I had been ravenous for touch. I knew that I would not be able to survive without it anymore. It was nourishing, intoxicating, and addictive. I would have to go with him. Or at least to where Human touch would be possible, and that left me only a few options.

"Will you meet with me again?" he asked.

The only response I had was to give him another kiss.

25

My heart was still racing when I left Reza. I tried to
shake off the fact that I could still feel his lips on me, his
hands on me, his eyes. I stopped and composed myself. As
excited as I was, I had to get things done. I went to the med
bay after trading a few favors to ask the doctor to take a
much-needed visit to the underguts to care for some sickly
dwellers, and then when I left I saw Caleb walking across the
atrium. He looked defeated, somehow smaller than he already was.

He stopped one moment to look up at the atrium ceiling,
with its faded painting of the early history of the then known
galaxy. Then he moved on. He did not try to barter badly
with the aliens outside of the Communications Hub as he
usually did.

I saw him go into the Sunspa. I finished my transaction
and then followed him in there. I did not need to bribe the
attendant to tell me which room he was in. I pushed open
the door of the G2V Yellow Star room, the star classification
of the sun that we circled back on Earth.

Caleb was in his briefs. His eyes covered with protective
goggles. He had his back to the door and music streaming in.
It was that song. The one that he was always playing on the
music player he'd procured for his bin.

"You're dealing with Jun wrong. You're soft when you should be hard. You cave when you should stand," I said.

That startled him. He turned to face me.

"What are you doing in here?"

He seemed embarrassed by his exposed skin. He dimmed the lamps to half and took off his goggles.

He put the towel around his waist and pulled on his shirt.

"You just need a little courage," I said.

"I've given up trying to talk to them," he said. "I'm never going to get off this station. I'm stuck here. We all are."

"You and Reza should talk," I said.

"Is that why you are here? Did he send you to convince me to take up with him? Go to Earth and join Earth Gov? Work from within?"

"No," I said. "I came on my own. I want to help you go where you want."

"Then give me the passes," he said. "I know you have them."

"I can't," I said.

"You're giving them to him," he said. "I understand. Reza always gets his way."

"No," I said. "They're useless. They're not passes off of here now. They'd be automatic death sentences. We all have to find another way."

"Where do you want to go, Tula? Not back to Earth. A girl like you can't go back. Where then? The Central Systems? A colony? Or will you wander?"

"I have to find Brother Blue, and when I do, I'm going to kill him."

Caleb took a deep breath in and then slowly exhaled.

"That's heavy," he said.

"He has to answer for what happened to my family. I don't know where that will take me after that. I may be dead myself."

"Accidents happen, you know," he said. "Whatever happened to your ship isn't necessarily because of him."

"Are you defending him?" I asked.

"I don't know what to think," he said. "He's done so much good for the people of Earth, saving it from the fate of so many other planets. He's well loved. He's been such a good person."

"He pulled off all of the grain from my colony ship and when I spoke up about it, he beat me until I was nearly dead and left me here," I said.

I could see Caleb struggling with what I had said. He had no reason to believe my word. I had no physical scars to show for what had happened.

"Maybe it wasn't what you thought," he said.

"What colony settles without its cargo? Without its grain?" I asked.

"But if you had those answers," he said.

"If I had those answers, I might want to kill him a thousand times over," I said.

After a minute, he put his hand on my shoulder.

"I believe you. And if I'm ever there when you meet him," he said. "I swear to you that I'll have your back."

"No," I said. "It's my load to bear."

The Sunspa timer buzzed, signaling that his time was up. The lights dimmed.

I swallowed, suddenly thirsty.

We made our way out of the Sunspa and purchased some waters and some essential salts. We didn't part right away. We lingered, as though we had crossed a threshold and were somehow more connected than before, even though we were not connected at all. We stood under the mural that depicted the beginnings of the Five Major Species. I pointed at the old map that depicted a history the galaxy had long ago moved away from.

"The map is always changing," I said.

I started to walk, and he followed me. We walked all over the station and then finally arrived at the warehouse where our robot was. I let him talk as he worked on the robot.

"The Imperium comes and sweeps all of the old ways out and they make judgments about which life forms should be held back, whose planets should be stripped, and which species they should lift. And if these species don't cooperate and get in the way of precious resources, then they and theirs are razed. The Imperium wants the resources, but it's only on the backs of what they call undesirable species that they send to barely viable planets that they'll get it. If you are with them, then you, your planet, your colonies, your species are protected. If you don't have a certain amount of colonies, then your life, your planet, are irrelevant."

"I get it," I said. "Brother Blue had the colonies. He's Earth's voice. If you integrate the colonies with Earth, then Earth's place would be even stronger."

"Those colonies are what give Earth a position. But everything that happened on our trip, it was as though we were never meant to reach the Children of Earth colonies."

"But why?" I asked.

"I know. It doesn't make any sense. But I can't shake the

feeling that we didn't have an accident. I think someone blew up our ship rather than let us get to our final destinations."

"Isolationists from Earth?" I asked.

"Maybe. I don't know who to trust in the Imperium or on Bessen. I don't know who to trust on Earth. That's why I can't agree with Reza. He wants to work from within and unite Earth, stop it from destroying itself or its chances for the future. But the rot goes too deep. If you pull out every piece, you're left with nothing. And then there's just chaos. But on the Rim, I could maybe sort it out. Have a fresh perspective. See the playing board in a different way."

The robot started to hum. It was turned on and moving forward and backward. Caleb had opened up its head and was programming command protocols. He executed one of them and music filled the room.

"Music?" I asked.

"It's essential. I'll be all alone on the Rim. I'll need something to keep me sane. And safe. I've built in some protection features as well."

"Impressive," I said.

"I'm good at what I do," he said. He took a rag and started wiping the robot, getting the dull parts of it to shine.

"The Rim is too far to do any good," I said. "It's pirates and loners and species with no power. Travel takes too much time to have any effect. You'd move one piece but by the time you moved another, you'd have lost your advantage. No, you must be central. You must bring the core to you. Reza is right. Earth is the way to go. Get Earth reunited, and then fight from there."

"Are you sure you're saying that because you think that? Or because Reza's got you all wound up in him?"

I blushed. Could he see the kisses on me?

"I don't have to take Reza's side," I said. "I can think for myself."

The robot was clearly agitated by my elevated voice. Its knives started whirring. Caleb gave it a voice command and the knives stopped and it shut down.

"I've programmed it to sense aggression around me," he said. "I can turn it off if you think you're going to start yelling at me."

"It thought I was attacking you?" I said.

"You are pretty angry with me right now," he said.

"Reza's right, you should go back to Earth," I said it quietly this time, even though the robot was powered down. "The two of you together could get something done."

He smiled.

"I don't see it that way," he said putting his hand on my shoulder again. "But Reza's a good guy. So don't break his heart."

26

Reza and I did not speak when we were together.
We lay together, sometimes kissing. His skin was mine. I
traveled farther looking in his eyes than I had to get here. I
took pleasure in simple things, hand holding, touching, and
sleeping in his arms. I had forgotten how touch could be so
rejuvenating. I was feeling so many things, all of them sweet
and terrible. I even found myself humming. I felt I could almost understand the word *belong*.

Our bodies had the conversations that we could not have.
Skin on skin. Lips on lips.

Relationships were so strange.

I almost didn't care about the hate that orbited my heart.

Although I was not ready to open my heart to happiness
completely, Reza and I were somehow bound together. I was
close to happy.

I did my rounds and then at the end of the day, I would
quietly slip into his bin. We did not make plans, we just both,
as though the rhythms of our days were in sync, would arrive
there at the same time.

Tournour made that more difficult. He seemed to excel in
showing up just as I was ending my rounds to go to Reza.

"Tournour," I said.

He nodded as one of his guards would take my bag and go through my things.

"You look impatient," Tournour said. "Are you in a hurry to get somewhere?"

I knew if I said yes, he'd keep me longer, so I shook my head.

"No. Take your time," I said.

Then Tournour dismissed his guards and slowly packed my things back up even though he could have confiscated it all. He started to chatter away about something he'd seen that he thought I'd find funny, or some entertainments he'd found exciting. Even though I mostly did find those things interesting, I could not concentrate on what he was saying to me because my body was too impatient to be with Reza.

"I've noticed that you're spending a lot of time with Reza Wilson. I just need to make sure you're not about to pull some trick like the communications array repair."

"Everyone was thankful about that," I said. "Except for you."

"It caused me a lot of headaches and work," he said as he handed me back my bag. "Well, I don't want to keep you."

I was already running down to the underguts where Reza was waiting.

It was a silent agreement between us that if we spoke too much then we would have to talk about the practical things. About revenge. About the civil war on Earth. About Brother Blue. If we ever spoke of the things that truly pressed up against us, our very real worries, our seemingly impossible plans for escape, our divergent hopes for the future, our bubble would blow apart. So instead I used this joy I felt to buoy me up. I allowed myself to fantasize that the passes were usable. That I could give him one so he could make his way back to Earth, and I could follow the pieces I was putting together.

As reluctant as I was to leave Reza's arms, I did my rounds every day, looking for a sign. And here it was.

It was an Imperium representative entering the Ministry of Colonies and Travel. I felt a rush as I tried to contain my excitement. I put my plans for trade on hold, and I waited to watch until the representative left the ministry. Soon, the passes might be usable again. I figured that I would follow him and see what his business was on the station. If I could determine it and whom he was dealing with then perhaps I could time it so that the passes I had would not be suspect. I could be days from leaving.

After an hour, he emerged.

The representative seemed out of place among the regular aliens moving about the square. His crisp uniform made him stand out. Everyone was careful to not walk to near him. He seemed agitated. Even though we were technically a part of the Imperium, once the census had been done, the Yertina Feray had been running itself without much interference from them. He flagged down an alien who looked up and pointed his tiny tentacle over to me. The representative nodded and began to walk toward me. I was not ready for him, but I could not escape now.

"Human, Human," he called after me.

"Yes?" I said. My hands started to shake as though I'd done something wrong.

"I am Ven Dar. You've been trying to reach me. And here I am."

He was a Loor, like Tournour.

I nodded. It was my habit to never deny what someone thought, even if they had made a mistake.

"I am very curious about the information you claim to

185

have, and I would be most grateful if we could meet in a discreet location to discuss the terms of your demands."

"Of course," I said.

Tournour walked by at that moment on his way to his office. The two Loor caught eyes and did an elaborate greeting. Then Tournour left without even acknowledging me.

"You know him well?" Ven Dar asked when he turned back to me.

"No," I said, surprised he asked since Tournour had so clearly ignored me. "But he's the chief constable. We've had dealings."

"But he . . ." Ven Dar said. "Never mind. I do not understand how these things work out here. Back home his greeting to me deferring power as his elder would indicate a close relationship with you."

"You're mistaken. Mostly he makes my life difficult."

"That must explain it," he said.

He seemed lost in thought and somewhat agitated. Ven Dar's antennae were darting about.

I wished that he would get to the business at hand. But I knew from experience that often times, in a deal, one must cultivate patience and indulge the client.

"An elder in his family must have done something terrible," Ven Dar said.

I'd never thought about Tournour having a family. But of course he must.

"Why would you say that?" I asked.

"It's surprising to see such a young Loor out in this part of space," Ven Dar continued.

"He's young?" I asked. I was surprised.

"Yes, barely thirty-five Loor years. I'd wager he's not even that. If I were to go by his shading."

"I thought he was old," I said. But what I did know about the Loor home world was that its orbit around its sun only took 212 days. Technically, Tournour was not that much older than I was.

"Oh, no. His family must be in great disgrace to have sent out their youngest. I would not have greeted him, but out here, one follows protocol. He's the chief constable, even if he is a shunned Loor."

I tried to digest what he had said about Tournour: a shunned Loor.

"Back to the business at hand. We do not suffer the slings of rebels lightly. You were wise to contact us to let us know what you had uncovered," he said. "My colleague—he is sorry that he could not come here himself, but it would be inappropriate and draw too much attention to the matter at hand—is willing to negotiate most favorable terms for your silence. I am authorized to reward you with your demands."

"I have so many demands," I said. From the amount of agitation this alien had, I could tell that whatever information he thought I had was very valuable and I could likely get twice what he thought my lowest demand would be.

"Well, we can discuss those once we speak in earnest. I'll let you know the location. I must make sure it is ideal. In a place like this, there is little that is up to Imperium standards."

"Of course."

He bowed and then left. There was only one other female Human on this station, so I knew that he had mistaken me for Els.

What was she up to? I'd likely been mistaken to keep her at such a distance. She was the one that I should keep near. I still had so much to learn. There was still time to pull her close.

27

. . . .

I didn't have to wait long to find out what was going on. Normally if someone came into my bin, I'd be up in a flash and ready to defend myself. But Els managed to sneak in somehow, quietly, without disturbing even the air.

I must have sensed something because slowly I came around and opened my eyes. Els was sitting there at my feet. It was the smell of the lotion that made me realize it was not a dream. She was dressed, as she always was lately, in extreme alien fashions. I marveled at Els's ability to incorporate the fashions of many different species and make it look good on her Human frame. She looked soft and sharp at the same time. Her mask of makeup was firmly in place, cheeks rouged, lips reddened. Els had grown wild. It was as though when the reality of being stranded on the Yertina Feray sunk in, it had made her go mad. She spent most of her time at Kitsch Rutsok's entertainments at night, screaming and cooing to anyone whom she thought would get word to the Imperium for her.

"What do you want? You're lucky I didn't kill you for sneaking in here," I said.

"You could never kill anyone," Els said.

"I would kill if I had to," I said.

"I have news," she said, ignoring me and instead grasping

both of my hands into hers. Her excitement was infectious. "Someone from the Imperium is here and wants to make contact."

Then she did that thing again, like she always did, where she seemed to summon tears up from nowhere. On Els, tears came when called; they did not spring up like a slow building storm.

"Yes," I said. "I saw a Loor representative from the Imperium on the main square."

"Why didn't they send a Human?" she asked. Her face darkened. And then she shook it off, as though it didn't matter. And then Els did that thing with her eyes that made everything seem like it *was* going to be all right. "What I have discovered is huge, they should respect me. I could bring down half the Imperium."

She was likely deluding herself, but she obviously had something of interest or Ven Dar wouldn't have insisted on agreeing to the terms she'd laid out.

"Really I have you to thank for it. Something you said to me made me realize something," she said. "Something big about Brother Blue."

"Me?" I said. If I had knowledge that could have harmed Brother Blue in any way I would have used it long ago. "What did I say?"

"That you never once were able to communicate with the colonies after you were left here," she said. "I've been going over the communication logs to the colonies that I had with me when I went into my escape pod."

"So?" I asked.

"I've spent every moment since then harassing aliens who have taken Humans on their ships. Not one of them was ever from a Children of Earth colony."

189

"Brother Blue felt they were too wild and wouldn't mix well with colonists," I said. It had been drilled into us colonists that the Humans who roamed and wandered were not to be mixed with."

"But don't you think it's strange? Not ever? No one from a Children of Earth colony has ever gone anywhere? And no Human who roams has ever settled on one of those Human colonies? Even on isolationist Earth, some people traveled. They had to for negotiations or for trade conferences. And exceptions are always made for immigrants when it comes to refuge. And now, thanks to Brother Blue's Children of Earth colonist effort, we're close to securing our place in the galaxy. There should be movement, communication, engagement."

I couldn't see what she was getting at.

"What's your point?" I said.

"There are no colonies," Els said. Then she bubbled with excitement. "It's all a con. Brother Blue has managed the biggest con ever. And I'm going to get myself in on it. I'm going to be one of the most powerful Humans in the galaxy."

I sank back into my pillow. As ridiculous as it seemed, something about what she was saying rang true. It would explain why Brother Blue didn't want us to ever talk to aliens. Or understand Universal Galactic or get the nanites. Or why the colonies had never responded ever to a single message I had sent, or if they did, with such strange and cold responses.

"Earth Imperium Alliance's whole position is dependent on those colonies existing," I said.

"Yes," Els said. "The Imperium only accepts Earth's status as a rising species because of those thriving colonies that Brother Blue built. And if that were true, and those colonies

190

were thriving, then my ship and I would be there helping them to reintegrate with Earth. But we didn't make it."

"And it would take a few years to retrain people and send them out to the colonies," I said, the truth of what she was saying dawning on me.

"With one ship exploding," Els said, "Brother Blue bought himself some more time to figure out how to stretch this con out, or wait out the Imperium. After all, things always fall."

"The map always changes," I said.

My mind was racing. We had him.

"But why destroy the *Prairie Rose*?" I asked. "We were a real colony ship."

"Probably because you were," Els said. "For the *Prairie Rose* it was just bad timing. Maybe he traded one con for another when the Imperium took control and changed everything. He could have used Beta Granade as a good front if he'd thought further down the line."

I shifted. He'd been grooming me. He'd wanted me to be a part of his plans. That's why I had to be eliminated. I knew it all, only I didn't know that I knew it.

"We should expose him immediately," I said. "That will get Earth united."

"No! I need Earth to remain where it is. The Earth Imperium Alliance is back in control there, and Brother Blue can't be doing this alone. There must be powerful people helping him with his secret. I got word to Brother Blue that I was onto him and in exchange for my silence and expertise, he'll get me a nice position on Bessen."

Els was diabolical. But she was going to get me closest to Brother Blue. He was within my grasp. The only way to find out was to play. I took a deep breath.

"How do you want me to help?" I asked.

I would have to pull her in closer to me so that I could best assess the situation and make a choice later on. If I alienated her now, I'd be in the dark and she was a wild card that I did not want out of my hand. Heckleck had always said to keep the wildest cards in your hand for as long as possible.

"I have to be sure that it's not a trick," Els said. "Will you pose as me for the meeting? You're still better at dealing with aliens that I am."

I nodded. She didn't trust her position. She needed a canary to see if the coal mine was safe. If it got me to Brother Blue, or to Bessen, to the Human embassy, with a knife in my hand, then I would do it.

"What do you need me to do?"

Els threw her arms around me. She squeezed too hard. When Els let me go, she withdrew a small data plug from her pocket.

"To show that my information is good, I'm to give the Imperium aide this."

"What is it?"

"It's enough to prove that my suspicions are real. He'll have to verify it."

She pressed the data plug into my hand.

"Once he does, then we'll head to Bessen together," she said. "You'll come with me."

I nodded. I would go to Bessen, but for different reasons.

"I'm going to have my life back," she said. "Isn't it wonderful?"

I wondered what it would be like to have my life back. I looked around at the cold white walls, breathed in the recycled air. The only home I knew on the station was the bin in the underguts on the Yertina Feray. As hard as life was here, it was a life I knew and it was not such a bad one.

Neither Reza nor Caleb could deliver me as close to Brother Blue as Els could. I would have to leave with Els no matter how detestable she was. She was my true pass out of here and toward my revenge.

"Tula. I will do anything in return for your help."

"Anything?"

"Anything," she said.

I knew from experience that no one would actually do *anything*. That was just something that people said. To give up anything was harder than one thought. There was always something that someone would not give up or trade. A thing that they couldn't do. I knew that everyone had that thing inside of them. I wondered where my line was. I was already willing to abandon Reza to follow Els to achieve my goal. What else did I have to give up?

"We're friends, aren't we?" she asked.

"What do you think?" I asked. I didn't know the answer to that myself.

"I don't know," she said. "I don't know anything anymore."

"I don't have much experience with Human friends," I said.

"I don't believe that's true," Els said. "You're friends with Reza."

"It's not the same," I said.

She brushed a strand of hair away from my face.

"Reza is so gentle," she said. "Is he gentle with you?"

I swallowed.

"I'm sorry. You know how boys are," she said. "They can split themselves so easily."

193

It hurt me that she implied that there had passed something between her and Reza. She was so slippery that I couldn't tell if it was just something that she had made up or if it was true. It didn't matter, it was an emotional blow and I wasn't used to them. It shook me, but I let it slide to stay in the game with her.

"I find him amusing," I said. "It doesn't matter."

"Of course you do," she said. "You know how it is. You should string him along a little longer. See if he has anything that we can use to secure our position with the Imperium."

"Of course," I said.

"Another thing," she said. "You'll have to keep those passes you have handy in case this goes wrong. We'll have to use them to escape quickly."

I struggled to keep my eyes locked with hers and to not look at the security panel where I kept them.

"When I first saw you, I saw that we had something in common. You and me, we're not so different. We're just two girls, far away from home. But you, you are special. I can see that about you."

Els had now moved in closer still. She put her hands on my shoulders. She kissed me. It was a warm kiss. Full of affection and softness. But it was so different from Reza.

"When I was young, all I wanted to do was to go to the stars. They would come up at night, and I'd gaze at all the places where I knew life was. I'd marvel at how sometimes a star that looked close was really far and on the Outer Rim, not near anything at all. That's how I felt, far away from everything. And now I'm here, and not in some slum on Earth staring up at the center of the galaxy, but nearly there."

She kissed me again. The kiss was electric, but it had no warmth to it. No love. She was trying to manipulate me, and to get what I wanted I would have to go with it.

"There is so much at stake," she said. "So much is going on that is bigger than you or me."

I kissed her back.

After a while we stopped kissing. I held her in my arms the way that I held Reza, but it was far from the same. I could tell that she thought she had me in her grasp.

"He wants to meet me at the Sunspa," Els said. "It's the only place where a meeting will raise no suspicion."

I was glad that it would be in public. I didn't want to do any of this in a dark secret place. If Brother Blue was involved, we were all in danger. But a place with a lot of light and many aliens was safe.

28

· ·

This Loor, Ven Dar, was nothing like Tournour.

His orange towel was ridiculous.

He came over to me as I stood by the refreshments. I made a big deal about trying to select the perfect kind of water to refresh me in the cabin. The pickings were slim and mostly high in minerals that I didn't like the taste of. I would have to settle for swill. I couldn't afford the high premium waters that I liked.

"I've heard that you have the large booth set to G2V yellow star," he said. "I'm here on official business, and I must get my time in. Would you object to sharing?"

"For a bottle of premium water?" I asked and indicated the bottles on the highest shelf.

"Of course," he said, paying for the most expensive bottle. I smiled. It was clear by his choice of water that Els had them very scared.

We made our way to the cabin, chatting. It was not uncommon for people to sit together in the Sunspa, every species needed their dose of sun. When the door clicked shut and we were alone, he got right to the point.

"Do you have what you promised?"

I took the data plug out. He took the plug and examined it.

"I'll be in touch," he said.

I was glad for the water; it was delicious. I finished it off and got up to leave.

I headed to Els to tell her that I'd delivered the goods. She was at Kitsch Rutsok's, surrounded by a group of aliens. I could tell that she thought that she had them wrapped around her finger. But she didn't see all the signs that they were trying to play her.

I slid into the booth and put my arm around her.

"How did it go?" she asked.

"Smoothly," I said. "They're scared."

"They shouldn't be," Els said. "I'm going to be the greatest thing that happened to them. I'm their ally."

Her sureness was so steady that even I almost believed that what she said was true. But I'd seen enough too good to be true deals go sour very quickly in my time, so I kept my reservations up front. There was always a catch. She would never believe me though.

"Still," I said. "We should be careful," I cautioned.

"Lighten up, Tula! The galaxy is about to drop into the palms of our hands. You should stop worrying and start celebrating."

She called over to the server to bring me a hot meal of fresh food. I knew she didn't have the currency yet, but in her mind she was already powerful and rich. Tonight, though, she would have to depend on the generosity of those aliens whom she thought she had twisted into owing her for her part in the communication array repair.

The aliens drifted off one by one, knowing that they could not pull one over on me. But Els was clueless, delighting in the fact that she thought that she had done well.

"I was meant for this," she said. "Meant to deal with different species."

"Yes," I lied. "You're so good at it."

"I'm going to shine bright on Bessen."

"I have no doubt," I said.

"You could learn a thing or two from me," she said.

She ordered a round of jert juice for us.

"Tell me what happened," she said.

"I gave him the data plug. He'll examine it and get back to us."

"It's such a bore that things take so long," she said. "I want to be out of here soon. Traveling to Bessen will take long enough, and I want to be living my new life already."

"Me, too," I said.

I changed the hours that I worked in order to avoid Reza. And I did not go to his bin. I wasn't sure if I could follow my own plan and leave him behind without revealing myself.

29

. . . .

I was surprised when Ven Dar came to me as I weaved through the third level only a day later. At first I didn't hear him because he called me Els.

"Els," he said. "Els."

He quickened his step until he caught up to me and then motioned for me to follow until we entered a private room.

"Let's get down to business," Ven Dar said. "Your proof could be a disaster for Earth and those of us who have been helping Brother Blue to keep up the ruse. You can't reveal too much or you and your people lose everything. We have you. You don't have us."

I started to protest. He put his finger up to stop me.

"But, we're willing to offer you amnesty on Bessen, and Brother Blue will offer you a position in his administration. He likes your initiative and thinks you may have something to offer. But it is determined that trouble may still lie with these Human boys. We followed up on your information that they have been dealing with disreputable characters. They were with you and they may know what you know. They are wildcards in our plan."

"They're harmless," I said. "They know nothing. I guarantee my life on it."

"I'm glad to hear it. But I've had instructions from my superior. The boys are too dangerous. They cannot live."

"You want me to kill them?"

"If you want to come to Bessen, you must dispose of them. We need to be certain of your loyalty."

"Leaving them here with no way off the Yertina Feray means they are as good as dead," I said.

I tried not to fumble the deal on the spot. Here was the anything that I would not do. I would not kill Reza and Caleb to further my own agenda.

"No," Van Dar said. "They could recruit people sympathetic to those opposed to the Imperium. The Earth Imperium Alliance has finally shifted back in control of Earth. But these boys could sway the population of Earth to Earth Gov's view to become isolationist again if they know about the colony situation. Better to kill them. Nip any rot in the bud."

"You want me to kill my friends?"

"From what you've revealed about them in your dossier, you are not their friend."

Of course. Els had been feeding the Imperium information about them to deflect any suspicion on her and to secure her footing with Brother Blue. She was ruthless.

"It will be difficult to manage without getting caught," I said.

I had to change tactics or Ven Dar would see that I was faltering.

"Make it look like an accident," Ven Dar suggested. "That always works."

"Of course," I said.

200

"We'll need to see the bodies before they are disposed of," he said.

"I'll arrange for a funeral," I said.

"Good," Van Dar said. "We expect that you will have a bright future in the Imperium."

He turned to go. If I was going to play a part in this heinous game, then I wanted something for myself.

"I have a question about the last colony ship. The *Prairie Rose*?"

He stopped and checked his datapad. His antennae waved slowly from side to side.

"The *Prairie Rose*?"

"It was a Children of Earth colony ship headed for Beta Granade," I said. "Just before the Imperium."

"I don't know anything about that," he said.

"But the *Prairie Rose* never made it there," I said.

"Well, someone is manning the colony," he said. "Each of the Earth colonies houses a small crew to help decoy and mask the lack of colony and to send messages and divert ships from there."

Someone *was* on Beta Granade.

"Could you find out who exactly is there?"

"Why?"

"I have a Human friend on the Yertina Feray. Tula Bane," I said slowly. "She was left here and her colony ship, the *Prairie Rose*, was destroyed on its way to Beta Granade. She wants to know what happened."

"Oh no. Another Human?" he said. "She'll have to be eliminated, too. No loose ends."

"No," I said. "She's with us."

It was strange to be defending my own life.

"Your word on this?"

"Yes," I said. "She's been helpful to me while I've been stuck here, and I'd like to give her some closure."

"I can do a search," he said.

"Thank you," I said. "I owe her a debt of thanks."

"Fine," he said, making a note in his datapad. "Will you do what we ask?"

"Consider the Humans dead."

He bowed to me and walked away. I had to sit down.

I would have to find a way to save Reza and Caleb by making them look dead.

30

In the middle of the night it dawned on me what I needed to do.

Poison.

Els was at the entertainments laughing with a group of aliens. They were a good time Minor Species, and Els had fallen in deep with them.

I dragged Els out of the party.

"What do you want?" Els said. "I was having fun."

"I met with Ven Dar," I said. "They're ready to agree to your terms."

"They are? We're leaving? When?"

"There's a condition."

"Whatever it is, I'm ready."

"We have to kill Reza and Caleb."

Els did not even blanch. She would kill them to get out of here. They were in her way.

"You'll help me?" she said.

"We need to make it look natural," I said. I couldn't kill Reza and Caleb. I wouldn't. But I had to make it seem as though I would.

"I thought that your attachment to Reza would make you queasy. I would understand."

I took her hand.

"I'm with you now," I said.

She smiled. It was the smile of someone who believed that they had won. Els hugged me and there was something in the hug that solidified the feelings that I had. Any doubt that I had about who I should help was swept away. Els created danger and chaos. Reza and Caleb were perhaps misguided in what they wanted to do, but they were good at heart. They believed that they were doing what was best for Earth, for Humanity, and, bigger than that, for a galaxy of aliens that they had not yet met.

"We don't want to get arrested for murder," I said. "We'll have to make it look like an accident."

"How will we do that?"

"Poison," I said.

It was hours before I could extricate myself from Els. Finally I did, exhausted and worried. As I made my way down to the underguts, I noticed Tournour was following me.

"I've been told to get a massive security detail ready for a high ranking arrival," Tournour said.

"Isn't that your job?" I asked.

"Yes," he said. "But these kinds of things don't usually occur on a small station like the Yertina Feray. Who is that Loor that you were talking with? Why does he refer to you as Els?"

"Tournour," I said. "I can take care of myself."

"You've no idea what you are playing at, Tula. These are dangerous times. Not many are who they say they are. Not many do what they say they will do. One hand distracts while the other slips a system into its pocket."

"In the end, good must win over evil. The trouble is trying to figure out which is which. Sometimes they look so much alike," I said.

"Tell me what is happening," he said. "Let me help you. I believe we've always been on the same side."

This was the moment that he was going to cash in all of the favors that I owed him during all this time I knew him. This is what he'd been saving them up for—a moment to do something big.

"I didn't know you were young," I said.

He frowned.

"I bear the burden of shame for my family by being sent out to make my way at such a young age. It's not something that I share lightly."

"You can't go home?"

"I thought I could when the Imperium came. My family situation had . . . *changed*. But I was wrong. I could not return. I didn't believe in what they believed in anymore. But it was better to stay here than to be killed for speaking out for what I believed to be right. I've tried to ensure that the Yertina Feray remained uninteresting to the Imperium. I tried to make it difficult for the Imperium to communicate their wishes with us. Alas."

I'd undermined Tournour's sabotage of the Imperium by helping Reza to repair the communications array. He'd been trying to protect the station, protect his own, just as he'd said when he interfered with my going on a ship for hard labor. Tournour was not the Imperium's man at all.

"So many things are wrong," I said.

He put his hand on my shoulder. It was strange, Tournour touching me.

"Tell me what's happening," he said.

His eyes were tender as they looked at me, and they were filled with genuine concern. His antennae were folded toward

205

me and even they looked sympathetic. I could trust him. Every bone in my body told me that I could trust Tournour.

"I need to make people seem as though they are dead," I said.

"The Humans?"

He did not look shocked or surprised. He was matter of fact, as though he were trying to best troubleshoot how to be able to help me.

"Two of them," I said. "But I can't let the other one know."

"What's your plan?"

"Poison," I said. "Once they are confirmed dead, I can revive them and get them off the station."

"Clever," he said.

"I think so," I said. "But timing will be everything."

"I'll need to be the one to find the bodies and sign their death certificates," he said.

I felt relieved. I was not alone.

"You do have those passes?" Tournour asked.

"I might."

"Keep them handy," he said. "I want to make sure that Heckleck's gift to you doesn't go to waste and that you have a way out of here."

I nodded.

"This isn't the first time that the Earth Imperium Alliance has wanted those Humans dead," Tournour said.

"You mean because someone sabotaged their ship?"

"I don't know about that," Tournour said. "It was those Imperium representatives that were killed. The chatter was that they were assassins sent to kill any and all Humans on the Yertina Feray. But of course Heckleck would never let them kill all the Humans here."

206

"So it's true. Heckleck killed those aliens?"

"He saved you," Tournour said. "But even I couldn't inter-fere with the repercussions of that. The bounty on him was too high, and he was not quick enough to use the passes and get off the station. I had to turn the other way. I hope he un-derstood. And I hope that by always helping you, he'll forgive me from wherever he is."

All the breath swooshed out of me, and I put my hand up on the wall to steady myself.

Everything was so much larger and more interconnected than I thought it was.

31

. . . .

"I've been looking for you," a voice said as I approached my bin.

It was Reza. He had been waiting for me. I knew that eventually he would come to me. Likely confused by my avoiding him. Everything about being Human worked in opposites.

"I'm right here," I said. But I knew that wasn't enough for him or for me.

"I saw you with Els," he said.

"Yes, she's my friend," I lied.

I looked at Reza. He was pained. Was he jealous that I'd been spending time with Els? All the intricate feelings made everything that I needed to do so difficult.

I took his hands and I curled my fingers around his.

"I have a plan," I said. "But you have to trust me. You have to trust that I know what I'm doing."

I wondered if a Human could ever sort out his feelings. It seemed impossible to know oneself. Here was Reza, standing in front of me, looking sorry and sad, and suddenly I did not know how I felt. Every emotion seemed unknowable.

"Quickly, come inside," I said. I didn't want to take any chance that Els might see us.

"Els is going to kill you and Caleb," I said. "And then she's going to Bessen to join Brother Blue."

"What?" he said.

"There are no Children of Earth colonies. That's why your ship never made it. If you had, you'd know that Brother Blue was lying."

"There are colonies," Reza said. "We just have to integrate them with Earth."

"No," I said. "They are ghost towns."

He scanned my face to see if I was making it up. He shook his head, then he cursed. I gave him a minute to sort it out in his head, to put the pieces together. Once he did, he would know it was the truth.

"Who knows?" he said. "Does Earth Gov know? This is just what I need to get them to listen to me and to unite instead of fighting among ourselves."

"I can't say," I said. "Els has recruited me to help her, and I am going to."

"You're going to kill me?" he asked. He looked horrified.

"No, I could never do that. I'm going to make you look dead," I said. "Once Els has what she wants, she'll be gone. We'll use the passes, and we'll go back to Earth."

"What it has come to seems so strange," he said. "We fought so hard to survive, and now we're all pitted against each other."

"No," I said. "Not Caleb. He'd work with you. He's still your friend."

"No. He's stuck in an idea that negotiations will not do."

"Why are you letting a difference of opinion come between you?" I said. "If you worked together, you could get so much more accomplished."

"It's not just politics. It's the galaxy that has come between us," he said.

"A galaxy is too big to get between people. Only small things can wedge themselves between friends."

But galaxy was exactly what got in the way of most things; it was even getting in the way of my heart.

"You'll give me the passes?"

"Yes."

"You'll come with me?" he asked.

"Yes. Yes. I'll go with you," I said.

I was surprised that I had lied to him. I had no intention of going back to Earth. My destination lay in the other direction. But I did not want him to hate me.

But it was true that I meant to go with him right now in this moment. With all of my heart, I meant that I would go with him despite my promises to the others. I was going to go straight to Caleb and offer him the same thing, and I would mean it that time, too.

I kissed Reza to reassure him of my intentions. If I spoke again, I would tell him that I was lying.

As I kissed him I could almost see me getting on a ship and trekking the months-long ride home to Earth. Just to be with Reza. But that was a path I could not take. Brother Blue was finally in my sights.

"But it's a secret," I said. "Els can't know that you know. You have to play along."

"Then I'll let you kill me," he said drawing me into his arms and sinking with me to the ground. "You have already slain me a thousand times."

32

. . . .

"Absolutely not," Caleb said.

He was near the docks, looking at the manifests for ships due to arrive, and we had already spent half an hour arguing.

"You have to," I said. "It's the only way you'll make it to the Outer Rim."

"Alien poisons are tricky," he said. "You might really kill me."

"I won't," I said. I'd arranged it with the doctor. I used every favor I had to get her to administer a slow working poison that would hit exactly when I pretended to poison them in front of Els. I explained this to him for the fifth time.

"Things can go wrong," he said.

"I have enough favors owed me to ensure that nothing will go wrong," I said.

"And you'll revive us, immediately afterwards," he asked. "No funny business."

"You'll wake up and be on your way to the Outer Rim," I said. "Ready to fight. Your way."

"I'll have to move Trevor down here so I can leave with him as soon as I wake up."

"Trevor?" I asked.

"My robot."

"Of course. That's not a problem," I said. "So he's done?"

"As good as. I just want to make as quick a getaway as I can as soon as I wake up."

"You will," I said. "I promise."

"And Reza?"

"He'll go back to Earth," I said.

"Does he know that you won't go with him?"

"No," I said. "Please don't tell him."

"We don't talk anymore," Caleb said. He looked wistful, as though he missed Reza and that no matter how he tried to couch it in his mind, a robot would not ever take the place of a friend.

He shook his head.

"You're some girl, Tula Bane," he said.

"I have to make Brother Blue pay."

"Forget Brother Blue. He'll do himself in. People like that always do. Come with me. A rebellion could use a girl like you."

"I can't," I said.

"I know you think that you'll go with Els and take care of whatever business you have with Brother Blue, but that is unrealistic. You'll be dead. They'll find you out, and they'll kill you. And if I don't like the idea of me fake dead, I definitely don't like the idea of you really dead."

"You can't change my mind," I said.

"I know I can't. That's what I like about you."

I smiled.

"If you succeed, what will you do? Where will you go?"

"Why does it matter?" I asked.

"Because when I'm off on the Outer Rim with Trevor and who knows what kinds of aliens, I'd like to have something

212

warm to think upon. I'd like to know where you'll be so I can imagine that you are all right."

"I suppose I would want to go planetside. Maybe somewhere that doesn't cause so much trouble."

"There is no such place," Caleb said.

"Quint," I said. "I'd go to Quint."

"But there is nothing there," Caleb said.

"There are flowers."

"You alone and a planet full of flowers?" He laughed.

"Everywhere has something that'll disappoint you. It's just choosing a disappointment and having it be the most tolerable," I said. "What about your girl, Myfanwy? The Outer Rim is far from where she is. Think of her."

"It's painful to think that she'll still have to wait."

"She's waited a long time already."

"Do me a favor," he said.

"Sure," I said. "But you'll owe me one."

"Tell her that I'm thinking of her," he said. "Tell her that I can't wait to see her again."

"I will," I said. "No charge for that one."

He smiled.

"Will you meet me at the med bay when I tell you to?" I asked.

"Yes," he said.

"Just don't tell Reza. He wouldn't understand why I can't go to Earth with him."

"My lips are sealed," he said.

The plan was in motion.

33

• •

A military disembarkment was an event. People flocked to the docking bay to see the pomp of it.

What I didn't expect to see was Brother Blue walking off the ship with a full security detail.

Brother Blue.

When I saw him, it was like being punched in the gut. My hands started to tremble. It was a powerful feeling. It was pure hate and terror mixed all into one. I wanted to rush and fling myself at him in a fury, but instead, I ducked even lower behind a pole, not wanting to be seen. I could not take my eyes off of him.

He was there smiling and talking with Ven Dar, his mind clearly not on past events. He was stepping onto the same space station where he'd kicked me to near death and his footsteps were careless, as though he were dancing.

I couldn't believe how ugly his face looked. I had remembered him as more handsome. I remembered his glow and his salt-and-pepper beard. I remembered his wide smile. But when I looked at him now, he did not glow. It was as though I could see the ugliness of his insides pouring out of him. He was grotesque in his finery.

He was escorted off the deck by Tournour. As soon as they were gone, I went straight to Els.

"Brother Blue is here," I said.

"My wishes have been answered. It's about time that they realized that I was not to be toyed with and passed off to a lower official. We're almost there. We have them now."

Els reached for my hand. I tried not to pull away.

It struck me that I was so far in deep with Els that if I showed how I really felt, she would kill me, too.

Every piece had to move perfectly. Every player had to be where I needed them to be.

They all trusted me. Now I had to trust myself. The plan was going to work.

First, Reza and Caleb made their way to the med bay where they got shot up with a dose of slow working poison, meaning that we had four hours before they would "die."

Tournour would have to be in the right place to find their bodies.

Els would have to confirm that it was them. The effects of the drug would wear off in twelve hours. By then, hopefully Els and I would be off the station.

There was a freedom to knowing that the plan would go down that night.

This whole thing was costing me every favor I'd ever accrued. I had traded too much for a corner table in the entertainment lounge, but it was essential.

I had to be there early, earlier than Els, Reza, and Caleb in order to set things up.

I felt awkward in the flow of the fabrics that I was wearing. I preferred the pants with hidden pockets I usually wore, not this silky shift. I liked my vest because it kept my breasts from being in my way, and from being exposed like they were now. But Els wanted me to look more feminine, and I needed to do what she wanted. I was already getting looks from the aliens in the entertainment center, unaccustomed to seeing me dressed so flamboyantly.

Els arrived and complimented my dress. She was extra excited. She was flushed. I ordered food and a pitcher of jert juice.

Caleb and Reza were late. I wondered for a moment if something had gone wrong in the med bay. Or if one of the moving parts of the plan had failed. I couldn't allow myself to think that.

But then they were there. They had arrived together, laughing and talking as though they were friends again, as though the fact that they knew they were on the same side against Els had united them. The enemy of my enemy is my friend. Each of them seemed to give me a secret hello, one that told me that they thought our relationship was the more special. They were all right, but for different reasons.

We ate food and we laughed. If I hadn't known that there were too many layers to the evening, I could have called it somewhat pleasant.

Els was calm. She nodded at me over and over again, as though she thought everything was going well. The poisoning was taking longer than I expected.

But soon enough Reza could not stop staring out the sphere window. He was deep into a third jert juice. And Caleb was staring at his hands. They were sweaty. Caleb's eyes were glassy and hard. At last I could see that the poison was beginning to take effect. I told the waitress to bring a bottle of low water. The water would help them when they woke up.

Part of me wished that Tournour would show up and nod to me that everything was going fine. I was so worried that I was going to fail. But he didn't. I had my part. He had his. I swallowed hard. I had to complete the plan.

I was in over my head. I could see that now.

And what if I was wrong?

I was playing with so many lives. We could all die and Brother Blue could walk away. That focused me back to the matter at hand. I could not fail.

Caleb's breathing began to be labored. It would soon be time to take them elsewhere.

The stars transfixed Reza.

"Can't see the sun," he said. "Can't see it."

I wanted to take his hand, tell him that it would be all right. I wanted to kiss his cheek. I wanted to crawl into his arms. I wanted to tell him how sorry I was that I wouldn't be going with him.

He turned his eyes on me. They were a deep brown like mud. They were bloodshot from the drink and from the poison now taking effect. Was his reaction normal? Had he been given enough? Too much? The waitress returned with the water, and I encouraged them both to drink it.

"You don't look well," Els said. "You should go lie down."

Els helped Reza, and it was up to me to guide Caleb.

He stumbled, and I held him up.

Reza and Caleb were slipping further and further away. I wondered if they would feel pain. The doctor had said the process of their systems slowing down would be uncomfortable.

Els suggested walking them all over the station until the

217

boys were confused and did not know where they were. I agreed because I didn't want her to notice any care on my part.

Els was whispering to Reza. And then she pushed him and he wandered away, stumbling down a corridor. I had told her to dump Reza, and then we would separate. I told her she should make her way back to the entertainments deck and sit there for two hours and make sure that she was seen. I had my own alibi to create.

I turned to Caleb.

"I'm uncomfortable," he said. "I feel rotten."

"You should go back to your bin and lie down."

"Yes, that's a good idea." Then he smiled at me.

"Saving the galaxy, to get my girl."

"Yes," I said.

"When do we leave?" he asked.

"Soon. You'll be down for nine more hours, and then we'll be gone. The passes will be waiting for you when you wake up. There's a ship headed to the Outer Rim a few hours after that."

"Thank you, Tula," he said. "I knew from the moment that I met you that you'd get me off of this station."

He turned and stumbled away. I watched him. He did not make it far before he staggered and fell.

I knew that his heart was slowing and stopping. I knew that his muscles were tightening. I hoped that the pain of it was quick. I unrooted myself from my place and ran to the arboretum. I felt like I'd plunged a knife into my own heart.

I went to my favorite tree and curled myself at its base. I hugged the tree and sobbed. I let the bark press into my skin.

The pain of it helped me to feel better. I hoped I had done the right thing.

In the morning, Thado awoke me. It was not the first time that he'd found me here asleep. He said nothing. He handed me a fruit and went about his business. He would be my alibi, and I would owe him.

34

· ·

It didn't take long for the boys to be discovered.

Els acted the part of hysterical girl brilliantly.

"But what happened! What happened!" she wailed.

She was clutching on to me in Tournour's office. He handed her a piece of cloth to wipe her eyes and blow her nose.

"It seems as though the boys had a night of hard drinking," Tournour said. He was looking at me when he said it.

"What will I do?" she screamed.

"It's hard to know what effect some of the more exotic drinks will have on a physiology," he said.

"I feel I'm responsible," I said.

Els shot me a look as though she thought I were going to confess to the poisoning.

"It's a shame they didn't ask you," Tournour said. "But that doesn't make you responsible."

She looked relieved.

"I feel guilty," I said.

"Nonsense," Tournour said.

"Did you want to have a memorial? Or can we just recycle the bodies?" Tournour asked. "I wasn't sure what kind of arrangements you Humans have."

"No!" Els yelled. "We have customs. We have rites we need to perform."

"Tell me what needs to be done," Tournour said.

"We need to have a viewing," I said.

"We'll help you make the arrangements," Tournour said looking at his datapad typing away. "But there is no room in Docking Bay 8 right now. We've had an overflow of travelers from that last Imperium ship. But we can set something up in Docking Bay 12 immediately."

"Thank you," Els said. She got up to leave. I stayed seated. "Tula, aren't you joining me?"

Docking Bay 12. I couldn't bear going back there.

"In a moment," I said. "I have business to finish."

The door clicked shut. I knew that she would tell Ven Dar where the bodies could be seen.

"Docking Bay 12?" I said to Tournour. "Can't you make it somewhere else?"

"Don't let a place define you," he said. "That was your past. Now let it be your future."

Then he clicked his communiquer and gave direction for the bodies to be moved to Docking Bay 12.

35

. . . .

Back to the beginning.

The last place in the galaxy that I wanted to go to was the hangar at Docking Bay 12 to meet with Ven Dar and Brother Blue.

No one was there except for the boys. They were lying in cryocrates. I put my hands on the glass tops. They looked almost peaceful.

I was glad to be alone in Docking Bay 12 to make my peace with the place before I saw Brother Blue face-to-face. I'd been preparing myself for this moment for as long as I could remember. As soon as he arrived I would confront him and I would kill him. I couldn't wait a moment longer. It would throw everything out of balance, but I didn't care. He would be dead.

I headed to the anteroom, a pilgrimage to where I had begun on this station. I noticed a crate in there, ready to be shipped with the word Trevor on its side. Even though he was boxed up, I was glad that my robot confessor was there with me in this difficult moment, just as he'd been there for me before. I could hear Brother Blue and Ven Dar talking as they arrived in the docking bay. Just hearing Brother Blue's voice made me shake. They did not see me in the dark corner. And to my surprise, instead of going to him and confronting him immediately, I crouched behind the crate that held Trevor.

Perhaps I was a coward.

No.

I would wait until Els arrived before showing myself. That was it, I thought. I just had to be patient.

Brother Blue's voice was so smooth and mellifluous when it poured out of his mouth. Most people would think that the tone was sweet. But to me, it was something awful. I began to shake even harder.

"So this girl, Els, who's been passing you the information, has a relationship with a Human that has been on this station since the *Prairie Rose* crashed?" Brother Blue asked.

"Yes, Brother Blue," Ven Dar said.

"I thought there were no Humans on this station. The records say there are no Humans on this station," Brother Blue said.

"Well, technically they say that, but apparently this one girl was left behind from a colony ship that was destroyed. No one claimed her. She was considered dead along with the others."

"The *Prairie Rose*."

"Yes," Ven Dar said. "That's why I've been asking about it. It seemed only logical to help get the information that they sought to smooth any suspicions she might have."

"And you've seen this girl with your eyes?" Brother Blue asked.

"I have not spoken to the colonist in person. But I've seen her from afar. The two girls are quite thick. The colonist helped to eliminate the two rebels."

"So the boys are dead?"

"Yes."

"How unfortunate for them. May their souls rest in peace. I will need to see the bodies."

"That's why we're here." Ven Dar said. I watched them as they walked over to inspect the two cryocrates. They seemed to believe the boys were dead. I breathed a quiet sigh of relief.

"Gentlemen," a third voice chimed in. It was Tournour. My heart leapt. I could face anything now that Tournour was here.

"You may take as long as you need to have a viewing, as I understand is your Earthly custom," Tournour said.

"I am satisfied that these Humans are deceased," Brother Blue said. "I'm glad that I happened to be on my way to Earth when this happened so I could see these traitors myself."

"Yes," Tournour said. "Fortuitous."

It was then that Els arrived.

"And this must be the Human girl, Els?" Brother Blue asked.

"No. It's the other one. From the colony ship," Ven Dar said.

I could see Tournour, from where I crouched. He did not correct Ven Dar. I should have stood up and shown myself, but my legs were rubber.

"Tula Bane," Brother Blue said. "You survived. If only I'd been carrying weapons then. But it would have looked bad to my followers. I see you've grown into quite the young woman. I almost didn't recognize you with all of that paint on your face."

"No, Brother Blue, you're mistaken. I'm Els," she said. "I'm the one who contacted you. I'm with the Earth Imperium Alliance."

"I'm confused. Ven Dar? Is this the girl you dealt with?"

"I have never seen you before in my life," Ven Dar said to Els. "Except for from afar, making arrangements with my contact, Els."

"I didn't want to arouse suspicion with my crewmates," Els said. "Tula and I swapped places. But now they are dead, and I can finally come forward."

Brother Blue called to Tournour, not trusting his aide or Els.

"Which Human is this?" Brother Blue asked Tournour. Tournour was looking at me, crouched in the anteroom between the two cryocrates. He turned to Brother Blue.

"I do not claim to be able to tell the difference between one Human and another," he said slowly.

"Where is the other girl?" Brother Blue asked, his voice rising to a vicious level.

"Tula will be here soon," Els said. I could hear fear in her voice. "She'll confirm what I said. We can trust her. She helped me to dispose of the boys."

"I thought I had cleaned up all my messes," Brother Blue said.

"I know it's confusing," Els said. "But I had to make sure that the boys weren't on to me. But now that they are dead . . ."

"Brother Blue, I can assure you that this is not the Human female that I did my dealings with," Ven Dar insisted.

"Let me ask you, child. What was the quarrel we had again?"

"I have no quarrel with you," Els said. "I want to be your ally. I had Tula bring the data plug to your man."

"Why are you asking about the *Prairie Rose*?" Brother Blue asked Els.

"I don't care about the *Prairie Rose*," Els said. "I just care about getting off of this space station and starting the new phase of my life."

"Ven Dar, you've been deceived. This is Els, not Tula Bane," Brother Blue said. "Tula Bane would never have forgotten our quarrel."

"I'm sorry, sir. You can see how she manipulated me. Humans are so tricky to understand," he said.

"Yes. We are," he said, and then turned to Els. "You want power. You want prestige. You want a place with me?"

"Yes," Els said. "I'll be an excellent asset to you."

"Too bad you weren't on the *Prairie Rose*. I could have used a girl like you back then, when the Imperium took over. Tula was such a disappointment."

"She's too soft for her own good," Els said. "We don't have to bring her along."

And there it was. It was unsurprising that Els would betray anyone in the way of her personal agenda, but it made me sad for her. It must be terrible to be so heartless.

"I agree. And I agree to all of your terms," Brother Blue said.

"Thank you, sir. You won't regret it," Els said.

"But it comes with a new requirement."

He removed a two-shot phase gun from his robe.

"That you are dead," he said.

A shot rang out. Els fell quickly and without a scream. More like she crumpled in a heap.

"Commander, what have you done?" I heard Ven Dar scream.

"I'm sorry, Ven Dar, you were a good aide. You've been indispensable. Very thorough, but I cannot have any loose ends about this."

And then there was another shot, and I knew that Ven Dar was dead as well.

I covered my mouth with my hand. I felt helpless. Tournour was in danger, and I had to help him. But I was paralyzed with fear. If I revealed myself, Brother Blue would kill me for sure this time.

"Where's Tula Bane?" he asked. I stood up from behind the cryocrate.

"There she is," Tournour shouted and pointed at me in the anteroom.

Tournour was now running toward me, he had both a phase gun and a knife out. Something in his eyes made me trust him. He fired two shots next to me, spending his clip and then stabbed me with the knife. But also there was that smell again. I was calm, and I knew to play dead.

"Well done, Constable," Brother Blue said as he walked toward us. "I really do love working with the Loor. You may recycle all of these Humans as you will," Brother Blue said.

I heard Brother Blue as he approached the anteroom. He crouched down close to me and stuck his finger in the stab wound to try to get a reaction out of me. It hurt more than anything and I nearly passed out from the pain. But the smell that Tournour was emitting seemed to get stronger and I relaxed into the calm and laid there like a stone. Brother Blue snorted in satisfaction.

"Finally dead," he said.

"Yes," Tournour said. I could tell that he was close by. I could smell that scent coming at me in a steady stream. I marveled at the fact that I was not dead, although I felt as though I had been somewhat drugged. "What a bloody mess. I'll have to file a report."

"It was an alien. You know how they hate the Humans," Brother Blue said.

"Yes, of course," Tournour said. "That's what I saw."

"But perhaps you want something," Brother Blue said. "For your troubles."

"Well," Tournor said. "It's been nice being ignored for the most part by the Imperium. I'd like my station to stay that way."

"Easily done," Brother Blue said. "I think that I can report back that things here are up to Imperium standards. No need to do another inspection for a long time."

"I'd be in your debt if you made sure that the replacement upgrades for the communication arrays were somehow lost or delayed," Tournour said.

"So we're done here," Brother Blue said.

"We're done."

"Well, then I'll be on my way. I'd like to get back to Bessen."

"Of course," Tournour said.

"I'll have to find a new liaison. What a shame Ven Dar got involved with this trash Human girl. She was his downfall. You Loors and your attraction to Humans."

"We're terrible that way," Tournour said. "It is a weakness."

Brother Blue grunted an acknowledgment and left.

A few moments later I felt Tournour hovering over me. He was pouring his emergency field med-gel into my wound and once the bleeding stopped, he brushed the hair away from my face.

"I'm sorry, I'm so sorry," he said. "Are you all right?"

"I'm not dead," I said. "I should be dead."

Now that Brother Blue had gone all of my courage came slamming back into me at once.

"Tournour, you let him go," I moaned. "You had him. You had him. Why did you turn the gun on me? You could have killed him!"

I tried to get up, but my legs were rubbery.

"I can still get him. I can still go. Give me your knife, Tournour."

"Tula, this is not the place to fight a man like that. And if I killed him there would be more questions, more problems. What we need now is someone to blame."

"Brother Blue!" I screamed. The pain was coming back. "Brother Blue was to blame."

"Brother Blue now thinks he's got a man here."

"He does! You helped him!"

The pain of the knife wound and of nearly having been electrified was making me hysterical. Despite the emergency field med-gel staunching the bleeding, I was woozy from the loss of blood.

"I told you, you and I, we've always been on the same side," he said.

My legs could no longer support me. I sank onto one of the barrels. Tournour released that smell again. It made my trembling and fear stopped. I felt calm.

"What is that?" I asked. "That scent."

"It's a thing that my species does when our partner is in danger, it calms when two Loor are bonded."

"I'm not your partner," I said.

"No," Tournour said. "You're not my partner. But I'm yours."

"I don't understand," I said.

"I couldn't bear the thought of him killing you, Tula."

I pushed myself away from him, away from the anteroom and into the main docking bay and put my hands on both of the cryocrates. I had made a promise to get Reza and Caleb off of here. But with this mess of death around us, the passes would never work. Tournour followed me.

I went over to Els's body and crouched over her crumpled form. I could see her gold bracelet, the one with Earth on it. I removed it from her wrist.

Tournour was standing a few feet away, looking at me like he was the one that was wounded.

As I looked at him, it struck me full on like a fire-hot point and then spread through me like a warmth that I had never known. He loved me. Tournour loved me. I thought back to every action he'd ever done, always kind, always consistent, always caring.

I had never been alone.

"Help me," I said going to him. I presented him my wrist and the chain, and he clasped it on for me.

"I couldn't let him kill you, Tula," he said. "And I know that your mate is Reza . . ."

"Shhh," I said. "I'm thinking."

I looked at the cryocrates. They had been verified as dead, so for all intents and purposes, they were dead. I remembered what Heckleck always said, that the dead can speak.

"Those travel passes are tricky things for people who are alive," I said. "But for the dead, well, no one cares about the dead who travel. They'll be angry at the way they traveled. But they'll be alive."

Tournour talked into his communiquer. "I've got a murder-suicide on Docking Bay 12."

He signed off and looked at me.

"I hope those boys wake up from their cryosleep to do some good where they are going. We who are against the Imperium need all the help we can get."

The rebellion was here. It was with Tournour.

Tournour then quickly gave instructions for the cryocrates and Trevor to be loaded onto two ships, one to the Outer Rim and one toward Earth. He zipped off an image of the passes to the correct authorities. Within seconds came the confirmation that the cargo had the authority to be loaded.

"Done. Your boys are safe."

I borrowed his communiquer and bartered favors that I had not yet called in to get the doctor to come down to fix my wound and dose the boys up on cryosleep for their trips, Reza to Earth and Caleb to the Outer Rim.

They would be angry with me, yes. But they would be on their way. I felt as though they were seeds of a sort and I was scattering them in the hopes for a revolution; each taking a chance to bloom in their remote part of the galaxy, in an effort to root out what strangled all life.

"I'm still stuck here," I said. "And Brother Blue is still alive."

"Don't be upset with me, Tula," Tournour said.

"He hasn't left yet. I can still go kill him."

"I won't stop you if that is what you want to do. But Brother Blue is a powerful enemy to have. You can't go after him alone. He would have killed you as soon as you moved."

I knew that he was right.

He looked at me and something had shifted. We were truly on the same side.

Instead of my life becoming harder and more unbearable, it was going to be easier. I took Tournour's hand, his fingers curled around mine. His hand felt warm, and I could feel the blood pumping.

I leaned into him, and he put his arms around me.

For the moment, we were the only two beings in the galaxy. Then the dockworkers came in to move the boys out, and his officers swept in to deal with Els's and Ven Dar's bodies.

"If I'm going to stay here, I want to go legit."

"You're going to stay? You're not saying goodbye?"

I nodded. Tournour was right, just as Heckleck had been before. There was a bigger game to be played here and that would take time and patience. To get Brother Blue to fall the hardest, to really make him suffer for all he'd done, I would have to wait. If I could make him fall a certain way, then perhaps the Imperium would follow.

"Legit."

"Legit?" he asked.

"Well, I can't be running around the underguts worried that I'll get thrown in the brig. Not if we're going to become friends."

He laughed and pulled me in tighter.

"What kind of hope does a Human girl like you have for a legit life on a space station with a shamed Loor who's in love with her?"

"I was hoping for a spot on the merchant deck."

"Really? What kind of establishment would you run?" he asked.

"I was thinking of dealing in sweets, waters, and salts."

"I'd have to have a chair always open to me. And I might like to have my items be on the house."

"Deal," I said.

"Yes," Tournour said. "Kitsch Rutsok could use a little competition."

"I'll call it the Tin Star Cafe."

We stopped to look out the window as the ships carrying Brother Blue and the boys went in their separate directions.

"One thing," Tournour said. "Eventually word will get to Brother Blue that you're alive and that the boys escaped. He will come after you."

"Yes, I know. But next time when he comes, I'll be ready for him. And he'll be the one left for dead."

There was no point in raging at the stars anymore. He was out there, and I was here, but now I knew it was up to me to change the map.

And I would.

Acknowledgments

• •

With kind thanks and much love to the following people:

My readers, Kara LaReau, Deborah Ross, Janni Lee Simner, Mary Williams, Kristen Kittscher, Sherri L. Smith, Shelly Li, Angie Chen, and Sangeeta Mehta.

My lovely brother, Laurent Castellucci, who spent hours talking Galactic Politics with me.

My narrative rock, Ben Loory, for listening to me ramble on about it.

My titler, Steven Salardino, always, always and of course Skylight Books.

My space science classes at Launchpad (apologies for all I got wrong here!).

My wonderful agent, Kirby Kim, who always thinks I can.

My amazing editor, Nancy Mercado, who helped me get to outer space.